Conversation Hearts

The Sweetbriar Mountain Series

Nora Everly

To my readers,
Happy Valentine's Day!

What happens on Valentine's Day
Stays on Valentine's Day.

Chapter 1
You mocha me crazy.

Holly

My sister was obsessed with holidays.

Even if they were total bull crap and manufactured by greeting card companies to make money off the desperate and lonely, it didn't matter, my big sister Violet loved them all.

"Aww, turn that frown upside down, Holly. Don't worry, be frappe-y! It's Valentine's Day and love is in the air! Can't you feel it?" Her maniacal laughter floated across the coffee shop, and I smiled in spite of myself. Had I mentioned she was now officially together with the love of her life and expecting a baby? *No?* Well, there you go.

The mood around here was cheery AF, and the coffee puns were never ending. Vi had finally got her happy back and her mood—while not quite infectious— was a joy to see. Nothing bothered her anymore, not even the lack of caffeine due to her pregnancy. It was a sight to behold. Like, I was happy for her. But, *come on.* Give a girl a break. Being single on Valentine's Day sucked.

"Smiling is not my favorite today, Vi. I deserve to be grumpy. I know I work for you, but as the last single sister in our little group of four, can I just say it's cruel that I have to hang up all this pink and red bullshit. Party or not, it's just mean." Not only had Vi found love, Lily and Rose, my identical twin older sisters, had too. "And that doesn't even get into how I feel about the cynical, corporate, manipulative way Valentine's Day is celebrated—"

"I agree, it can be a bit overwhelming, and corporate and whatever, but that is irrelevant. I just want to eat chocolate and dance at my party. Cheer up, for me? Pretty please? I'll bring you a pound of See's Candy tonight. I'll be your Valentine, Holly. You don't need a man, I promise."

"I know I don't need a man to be happy. I'm totally happy and content. I'm delighted as hell to be back in Sweetbriar, okay? It's just *this day.* I'll always be on edge on Valentine's Day. And for the record, I'm not fragile. I know what all of you think of me—"

"*Ugh,* you're right, I'm sorry. I was hoping my party would make you forget about *him* and *that* and, uh, you know, just for a little while..."

"I practically left him at the altar, Vi. One doesn't forget such things, okay? The guilt alone is enough to make me want to hide under my covers. The entire month of February is basically cursed for all eternity for me. I don't want to talk about this anymore. And I will be expecting the See's."

"It's time to forgive yourself. You should just talk to him." An emphatic hand slapped the shop counter. "You didn't '*runaway bride*' him, you left him a letter and then you left town for what? Ten years so he wouldn't have to run into you in town? Plus, he's married now and happy too, he has five kids, Holly. And don't worry about the See's. I have a few boxes at home, for emergency chocolate cravings." A slow, secret smile traced over her lips. "Jake picked them up for me when he was working at his Portland office last week."

I shook my head. "Girl, do not let him get away." I stopped my petulant pacing and returned to placing rosebud filled vases on top of heart-shaped doilies on top of Violet's pink tables.

"I don't plan on it. We're getting married ASAP—probably at his cabin. So, don't make plans for any weekend in the next month."

"Way to be specific, Vi. But you're in luck. I have zero plans and zero possibilities of making any if it's not with someone who would be at your wedding."

Her mouth quirked up in a smile. "Perfect." Maybe I should let her good mood lift my spirits.

Violet owned the best coffee shop in Sweetbriar, Oregon and tonight was her annual Valentine's Day mixer—otherwise known as her night to shine as one of the town's most notorious matchmakers. Because of her pregnancy, she was taking it easy at work and as her temporary manager, I had to be here tonight, like it or not

—and I didn't. I was also the lucky sucker to add the finishing touches to the party décor. This place was brimming with hearts and flowers, love, good cheer, and pastel balloons designed to look like those ubiquitous candy conversation hearts. *Blech.* It was almost closing time, and the shop was empty, so I was free to go full grouch.

"Is there a Valentine's Day equivalent to mistletoe?" she asked while aiming a quizzical smile my way.

"I don't think so. I guess we could tell people to kiss under the conversation heart balloons—" I let one go and it floated to the ceiling. "What do you think? The ribbons dangle down, just like mistletoe."

"Love it! I'm going to write it on the chalkboard outside."

"Wait. Are you sure about this? People are lonely on Valentine's Day and horny too. Do you really want to encourage that kind of vibe tonight? Like, people might try to hook up in your bathroom, or sneak into the back room."

"This is Sweetbriar! No one will do that. It's just innocent fun. It'll be fine."

"Freakin' awesome," I muttered. On the bright side, I no longer had to arrange the balloons artfully, they were now free floating up against the ceiling with their ribbons hanging below, just waiting for some poor fool to wander beneath.

Her hands hit her hips. "Oh, come on. Do you want to fall in love again? Everyone wants to find love, right? It's universal." She huffed with her head tilted in mock annoyance. "I could help you with that if you like. I'm very good at what I do, as you know. And if you doubt me, I can point out all the matches I've made when they arrive at my party tonight."

"I'm not ready for that yet. But you know what? I've never been in real love. I know it now. Maybe someday I'll be as giddy as you are. Never say never, right?"

"That's the spirit!" Her eyes drifted past me to the shop's front door. "Rethink the 'not being ready' thing for me. How about today? It's Valentine's Day, please?" She pressed her hands together, pleading with me like a kid.

Ding.

"No," I mouthed, shaking my head. "No way. Not today." We were in the rear of the shop, in the corner by the sofa and my back was to the door. Thankfully, he was out of earshot.

"*Gah!* You're such a big poop." Her teasing was affectionate. I knew she wouldn't push me into anything I wasn't ready for.

"Nice, Vi. It's him, isn't it?" I hissed as my breath caught and my pulse raced out of control in anticipation of a Liam dopamine hit. I fought the urge to run to the bathroom mirror to check myself before he could see me.

"When you get home, you need to meditate, recharge your crystals or burn some sage, whatever it is you do to adjust your aura into a better mood for the party. It's just a day. It doesn't mean anything. I'm only half making fun of you by the way—and yep, it's him."

I shivered with the knowledge that my favorite eye candy was in the doorway. "Very funny," I whispered. "But now that you mention it, Mercury *is* in retrograde, and my favorite rose quartz pendulum has gone missing—"

"Good afternoon, ladies. You're open, right?"

"Yep, and you're always welcome here even when we're closed, Liam. The usual?" Vi asked as she strode to the counter.

"Yes, please. Hey, Holly."

"Hi." I had to hold in my sigh as I turned around to greet him.

His eyes drifted around the shop. "It looks great in here. Can I do anything to help?"

My eyes longed to wander but I managed to hold them steady on his face, which was not easy because Liam was a sight to behold. He was six feet six inches of heavily muscled former Army Ranger hotness and I swear, he was so damn sexy he smoldered.

I had met him a few months ago when I came back to town—long story—and had been not-quite-crushing on him ever since. If I allowed myself to talk to him for more than five minutes at a time I'd definitely have it bad (okay, dang it, *worse*) for him. I'd been lusting after him for months, along with every other single woman in town. He was just too good-looking to be real.

"Did the balloons get away from you?" He reached up and snagged a ribbon. "Need help getting them down?"

Violet turned from the rear counter where she was preparing his latte. "Nope. Think of the balloons like mistletoe. If you end up under one with someone, then you have to kiss."

"Ahh, I see." He answered without looking at her, he only had eyes for me today, it seemed. "But not until tonight, right?" He handed me the balloon with a wink then turned to meet Vi at the counter.

"Right..." I breathed. *Hot damn.*

With a shake of my head, I let go of the ribbon and rushed to Violet's office to hide and *not* create another elaborate Liam fantasy in my head. I needed to gather my wits if I was going to survive the party without giving him the wrong signals.

Chapter 2
Where have you bean all my life?

Liam

Maybe one day I'd ask her out. But today was not that day. The thought that I shouldn't even try with her held me back. Nerve or lack thereof had never stopped me whenever I was interested in a woman in the past, but Holly was different. My best friend was married to her older sister. And while he wasn't related to her by blood, they'd grown up together and he'd always been a big brother to her. A guy was supposed to stay away from his best friend's little sister, or in this case, sister-in-law, but that wouldn't matter to Luke, he was protective no matter what. Plus, over the last few months, I'd grown close to her family, they'd taken me in like one of their own, and putting that at risk would be stupid.

But, damn, she was gorgeous and the brief glimpses I'd seen of her personality whenever I could get a word out of her had me intrigued. She was funny and cute. I couldn't help myself, I wanted to know her better.

Why did I have to meet who could quite possibly be the perfect woman for me now? I didn't have any business being with her.

Violet's voice startled me out of my morose thoughts about her sister and I flinched. "You're coming tonight, right?"

"Huh?" Holly's nearness had me flustered, like usual.

"To my party, silly. You'll be here tonight?"

I shot her a grin. "Wouldn't miss it, Vi." Yeah, only because I knew Holly would be there. Otherwise, hell no. Being around a bunch of people on Valentine's Day as a single guy was not my idea of a good time, in fact, it sounded like a nightmare.

"Yay!"

The warm glow of Violet's good mood buoyed mine and I let out a chuckle. "I'm glad you're so happy. You deserve it."

She turned serious. "You deserve it too. Happiness, that is." Her eyes flicked briefly to Holly as she came through the swinging door that led to the back of the shop. "And I've made it my mission to see that you get it."

An array of feelings skidded through my mind at her words, running from thankful to trepidation—*was she planning something?* I chose to settle on thankful. "Thank you. You're one of the people who have made me feel at home in Sweetbriar, it means a lot."

"Good. I hope you know you're never leaving. You're one of us now." She slid my takeout cup and bag across the counter. "I'll see you tonight. Wear something pretty," she teased.

"I'll do my best. Bye, Vi." Unable to help myself, I turned for one more look at Holly before I left. "See you later, Holly." I almost winked but ended up hiding it behind an excessively long blink which probably made me look like an awkward freak.

I crossed the parking lot to my office, shaking my head along the way. *Not* flirting with her was getting more and more difficult, almost impossible.

"Hey," Luke greeted me as I entered the building. The office for McCabe Construction was where I'd spent most of my days since arriving in Sweetbriar. Luke and I were Army buddies and both medically discharged after we had fallen under attack in Afghanistan. He hired me at his family's construction business, giving me a direction I'd desperately needed, and I'd been here ever since.

"If I'd known you were still around, I would have grabbed you a coffee too."

"No worries. I have to head home and get ready for Vi's party. Lily wants us to coordinate our clothes."

I raised an eyebrow; he did not look even one bit annoyed at the prospect of wearing matching outfits with his wife. "You're cool with that?"

He shrugged with a grin. "Don't tell anyone, but I'll do anything for that woman, and I don't give a shit what it is either. If she says jump, I'll ask her how high and if I can grab her a drink on the way down. So no, I don't mind. Besides," a slick grin spread across his face, "she likes me in a suit. She probably just picked up a tie to match her dress or something. No big deal."

My brows drew together. "We have to dress up for this?" I had a suit, I hadn't worn it in forever, not since my grandmother's funeral, but at least I owned one.

"It's a mixer, dude. Dancing, champagne, no kids will be there, shit like that, so yeah, definitely dress up. Oh, and warning—Lily said Violet uses it for recon. She likes to meddle."

"Meddle?"

"She's a matchmaker, just like her mom. One thing you have to know about this town is it's small, people are nosy, and Violet and Dahlia are the worst out of all of them."

"Great," I muttered, sipping my coffee.

"I'm married and loyal. *I* have nothing to worry about. *You*, on the other hand? Single, former Army Ranger with an addiction to working out—" His mouth quirked with humor. "How tall are you again?"

"Six, six," I grumbled.

"Oh yeah, you're doomed," he declared. "It's only a matter of time before they start trying to fix you up."

"Fucking great..." I repeated.

"It'll be all right. I'll have your back like always."

"Thanks, man. I appreciate it but this is not quite like one of our missions back in the day."

"It's still no problem. You come find me and Lily tonight if they try to force you to dance with one of Vi's hot friends and we'll protect you."

I flopped back onto the lobby's sofa and tossed my takeaway bag on the coffee table. "You're hilarious."

His eyes were alight with sympathy when they met mine. "Seriously though, you've had a tough year. Come find me anytime you need me. I mean that."

"I know you do, and I swear I'm almost past the doom and gloom. I'm feeling much better—"

"You know there's no rush, right? We're going to have plenty of good days but it's okay to have bad ones too. I told you coming here would work out for us. Now, tell me I'm right, you know how much I like to hear it."

"You were right," I admitted with a chuckle. "About everything."

"Stick with me. We're going to be fine. I'll see you later on." He flicked out two fingers in a wave then left.

I should go home and get ready too. But I found myself mindlessly sipping coffee and staring out the window instead as I thought of tonight and how I should be around Holly. And wondering why I had to be so hopelessly interested in a woman I could never have.

It was safer to stay away from her entirely, I decided as I made my way outside to my car to leave.

Chapter 3
Relationship status: It's caffeinated.

Holly

"Yo, Holly is that you?"

"Yeah," I shouted as I slammed through the front door of my twin little brothers' townhouse. I felt like such a loser for couch surfing with them. They had it together far more than I did, sure they couldn't cook worth a damn and were always mooching meals at our parent's house, but they were gainfully employed as firefighters, and they had their own place which was more than I could say for myself at the moment. "Jude?"

"Nah, he's at work."

I followed the voice to find Levi in the kitchen—and okay, my brothers weren't "little" anymore, just younger by a little over a year. Since age twelve, they had each towered over me by at least six inches. "Are you going to Vi's tonight?"

"Hell no," he muttered, popping his head out from behind the refrigerator door. "You should go to the store. I never know what to buy and we are out of everything."

I shrugged. "Get whatever you like to eat, duh. Just because I'm a girl doesn't mean I know how to cook. And, hello? Vi's gonna be pissed if you miss her party."

"Don't care. And I like to eat home-cooked food, like, I don't know, lasagna or a fucking meatloaf or something. I'm getting sick of sandwiches and frozen waffles. I don't know shit about ingredients."

"Well, I can't help you. I made friends with the food carts when I got back into town and it's getting pretty serious. I might actually be in a relationship with the fish and chips truck."

"Oh yeah?" He smirked and I braced myself. That smirk had always meant he was about to drop an information bomb of some kind. "I heard you'd rather be in a relationship with Liam."

My heart raced in alarm. "*Pfft*, no. Who said that?" I scoffed as I tried the casual approach. Levi had a strange ability to read people and I knew he'd figure out exactly how much I was interested in Liam if I gave him even half of a clue to go on.

"Little birdies named Lily, Rose, and Violet—our sisters. I think Mom may have mentioned it once or twice, Gram too and maybe Aunt Delphine and the cousins. In other words, watch your back tonight, you know they'll be scheming to get you alone with him."

"*Ugh*, frick. You're lucky you can skip it. Violet gave

me a job at the shop, I owe her. I can't skip out on her; it wouldn't be right. But, my god, Levi, she has the dangling balloon strings acting like mistletoe for eff's sake. She's in a love haze now that she's with Jake. Since she's happy again, no one is safe until the entire town is happy right along with her."

"There will be no single person left to complain with after tonight if she has her way."

"Right?" I looked at him expectantly.

He shook his head. "I'm still not going."

"*Dammit!* Fine. I need a buffer, Levi. Come on, please? I'll learn how to make Mom's chicken pot pie, just for you..."

"Sorry, can't do it. I have big plans, nothing but Netflix and probably pizza delivery is on deck for me tonight, maybe I'll go to bed early, who knows?" His mouth spread into a snarky grin. "And we both know Marie Calendar makes Mom's chicken pot pie. Even I can put frozen shit into the oven."

"*Ugh*, Fine." Fully regressing back to our childhood, I stomped my foot. "You're so lucky."

"Am I?" His eyes became unreadable before he turned away.

"Oh, Levi..."

"Have fun tonight, Holls."

"Okay, but if you need to talk..."

"I don't. I'm good." His smile was not convincing, but I let him go into the living room without pushing him to spill his guts. I mean, I didn't want to be pushed about my own feelings, why would I push someone else into speaking about theirs?

"I'm sorry," I called over my shoulder as I headed into the bathroom to get ready for tonight.

"No worries," he shouted back. "I'm fine."

Fine. Yeah, right, If he was fine like I was fine, then we probably should just stay here and talk out our problems with each other tonight.

Alas, I did not have time for feelings and wise decisions. If I wanted to look hot tonight, I had to get started.

I stopped with my hand on the bathroom doorknob.

Should I?

Would Liam like it if I wore a sexy dress and did myself up?

Did I really want to look hot and risk—?

But was there really anything at risk? Or was I stuck in a one-sided crush?

Who was I kidding? Of course, I was going to show up looking hot. Life without risk was boring. Shoving the door open, I shrugged at my reflection in the mirror. I tried to wipe the cynical frown from my expression as I studied my face.

Cat eye, bright pink lips, and beachy waves. I decided as I turned on the taps to fill up the tub. *A tight dress, high heels, and lots of cleavage, no wait, lots of leg instead...*I had the perfect minidress, hopefully, it wasn't wrinkled, I was living out of a suitcase here. I added bath oil to the water as I added to my running list of hot-girl essentials I needed for the evening. Maybe I should wear some lip gloss, if he kissed me under a balloon, I could turn his mouth pink and leave my mark on him.

With a sigh, I slid into the hot water, letting it wash away my trepidations. I should try to have fun tonight. I deserved a good time; I'd freaking earned it. And everyone knows, just like Vegas, what happens on a holiday, stays on that holiday. Maybe I'd cash in my holiday hall pass this year and get a kiss.

Or more than a kiss? I shivered, unable to deny the spark of excitement at the prospect. He was sexy with clothes on, so tall, so many muscles... I shut my eyes and allowed myself a moment to picture him without.

Gah!

Why do some decisions have to be so hard?

Or more to the point, why was the *right* decision so hard to stick to? I was not in a position to get involved with someone right now, not when my life was so unsettled. I was living with my brothers. Who in their right mind would want to come home in the morning after a hot date and be faced with their little brothers? No one, that's who. Not to mention the fact I could never bring anyone home with me, not until I could afford my own place. Which in Sweetbriar would be never. I'd need a roommate or a winning lottery ticket to afford even a studio apartment. Violet paid well, but let's face it, part-time at a coffee shop was not going to be enough and I was through with my travel blogging days. That money had run out months ago.

I pulled the plug in the tub and then grabbed my robe. "I'll be in Jude's room getting ready."

Of the two, Jude was less messy. He let me keep my suitcases in the corner of his closet. Stepping through the doorway to the small room, I considered moving back to my parent's place but rejected the idea immediately. My mother was just too nosy to live with.

Blowing out a sigh, I dug through my clothes until I found what I needed. *Long-sleeved black body-con LBD, cut to mid-thigh.* It would be cold tonight, but who cared about that when I had Liam to impress? Losing myself in my fantasies, I let my imagination take over as I applied makeup and styled my hair. After slipping into a pair of four-inch black stilettos with little rhinestones near the toe, I grabbed my coat and bag and headed into the living room.

Jude had come home along with his friend Harper and her daughter Bella. "You look so pretty!" Bella got up and ran to me. She was about six years old and cute as a button. "You have princess shoes on! Can I wear them next time I come over?" She turned to Jude with an accusatory glare. "Your sister has diamonds on her shoes! Why didn't you tell me?"

It had been ages since I felt this good about myself. I couldn't help it; I beamed at her and twirled in a circle. There was something awesome about impressing a little kid. "Thank you! Of course, you can. And I have more than just these too. I'll dig them out of my storage unit and show you. You can play dress up if you want."

"Really? Do you have purple ones? Purple is my favorite color, just like my almost, great auntie Violet."

Harper was Vi's fiancé Jake's niece, so she would become Bella's great aunt when they got married. Sweetbriar was just a small town after all.

"Yup, I'll bring them and some more dresses and put it all in Jude's closet."

He shook his head with a good-natured smile. "Great, I look forward to not being able to find my clothes."

"Don't be a poop, Jude," I scolded. "It's for Bella." *And for me.* I missed having a full wardrobe to choose from. "Your closet is half empty anyway. And why aren't you guys going to the party tonight?"

"We have Bella to take care of." He shrugged. "And go ahead and hang your stuff up, I don't mind."

"Thanks. Well, I'm off. I guess." Uncertainty washed over me, and I hesitated in place. I should go change into something more—well something different. This outfit was too much.

"Uh-uh, no. ma'am, you are not. Hold up. Wait." Harper stood and led us to the front door. "Girl, do you have extra plans for tonight I need to know about?" She lowered her voice to a whisper. "Do you need to use my place?" I'd known Harper since we were little kids. She'd been best friends with Jude forever, we were also close.

"Gosh, no. But I appreciate the offer. I—I don't know what got into me, I guess I just felt like looking nice for a change." I shrugged. "I—"

Harper's eyes lit up with sympathy. "I get it. Being lonely sucks, doesn't it? And starting your life over is hard."

"I mean, I'm not a tragedy or anything. I just needed a change. Drifting around for the blog wasn't working for me anymore, you know? It's time to put some roots down again."

"Well, I for one, am so glad you're back for keeps. I missed you. Sweetbriar wasn't the same without you."

"I missed you too."

"Plus, let's face it, that Liam is certainly a hot one. I can't blame you for—"

"Hold on." Caught off guard, I stiffened. "Wait a minute. Stop. What are you on about? Liam? I don't—?

"Ohhhhh." Her lips pressed into a line as she fought laughter. "This is what we're doing. Gotcha." Her nod was sage as her lips quirked into a knowing grin. "The denial stage."

I blew out a semi-annoyed, semi-exasperated breath and shook my head. "You're a nut, Harper."

"Have fun tonight, Holls. We'll talk about this later." She waggled her fingers at me as I slipped into my coat.

"Whatever, dude. Have fun with my brother tonight. Maybe we'll talk about *that* later too."

"Or maybe we can do the Sushi truck for lunch tomorrow and talk about everyone else instead?" She suggested with a light shrug.

"Add some Sake and make it dinner and we have a plan."

"It's a date." Her mouth turned up with humor. "Bring your heels to my place to distract Bella and we'll hang out."

"You got it." I hugged her and then headed to my car.

Minutes later I found myself sitting in my car in my spot behind Violet's shop questioning every single decision I had made since I had gotten home. I couldn't go in there like this. What had I been thinking? I was dressed for a night out at a fancy club, not a small-town coffee shop Valentine's Day mixer. Jeez.

Fingernails tapping on the top of my car sent my heart racing. "Oh my god, you scared the heck out of me, Violet!" I cried as I opened the door and got out.

"Oh, girl! Look at you." She flicked one side of my coat open. "It's the infamous black dress, Harper told me you were wearing it. You're freakin' stunning, I'm so jealous of your legs. I love it! Come on, Jake is waiting inside, we're just getting started." She took my hand and tugged me toward the open back door. "I have a co-host for this party and I'm going to dance my ass off tonight! Woo hoo!"

"You are on another level of happiness, Vi. You're transcendent and glowing and gorgeous. I have never seen anything like it."

"I know, isn't it great?"

"It really is. I'm so happy for you."

"I'm happy for me too. Finn and Nick are even here!" Her twin sons had never attended this party before. They'd just turned seventeen, I guess she felt they were old enough.

"Oh good, I haven't seen them since Mom's Sunday dinner last week—"

"Violet, come out here and dance with me, gorgeous."

We heard the deep echo of her hubby-to-be call out from the front of the shop.

"It's Jake!" She beamed at me. "You look brew-tiful, Hollyberry, have fun tonight."

"I'll try my best, words cannot espresso how happy I am to be here," I deadpanned.

"Yay! You finally coffee punned and it's a good one! I'm totally putting it on a shirt." She dropped my hand like a hot potato and went flying through the double swing doors leading to the front of the shop to dive-bomb Jake.

"Catch you later," I muttered. "Don't worry about me, I'm totally fine..." Laughing to myself, I opened her office door to stow my bag and coat inside.

"Hey."

"*Gah!*" I spun in the doorway to find my older, but tiny redheaded twin sisters, Lily and Rose standing on the other side. They creeped me out sometimes with their spooky mind-meld and affinity for acting like those weird twins from *The Shining* to freak our brothers out. "Quit looking at me like that." I waved a hand in front of myself to ward off their heebie-jeebie vibes.

"Chill out, Holls. We're not doing anything." Rose laughed.

"Speak for yourself." Lily side-eyed her. Then moved her unblinking dead-eyed gaze to mine. She didn't look away until I flinched and took a step back. Her sense of humor took over and she laughed. "God, you're too easy."

"Whatever, Lil. You're scary sometimes and you know it."

She shrugged. "It's a blessing and a curse. But seriously. Mom's here and she's up to no good. Remember Jared Jamison? From back in high school."

"Uh, yes. I remember him." He had asked me to the homecoming dance all four years, and it hadn't mattered to him that I had a boyfriend all through school either. He was persistent but not in a rude way. He'd always struck me as cute and kind of innocent, a nice guy.

"Well, he's here and Mom wants to fix you up with him."

"Isn't his dad the mayor now?"

"Yep," Rose answered. "And she's besties with his mom too."

"*Blech*," I grumbled. "He's nice, but I'm not in the mood for this right now."

"That's why we snuck back here, to warn you." Rose lowered her voice, being purposefully mysterious.

"Yeah, creeping you out in Violet's poorly lit back room was just a bonus," Lily nudged my side.

"Glad I could amuse you,"

"Rosalie!" The booming voice of Rose's hot-cop hubby rang through the air.

"It's fine," I teased. "Go on. Don't worry about me."

Lily laughed. "Aww, don't worry I'll keep you company. Luke and Liam are at a table in front, we'll go up and sit with them."

Trevor pushed through the door brandishing the ribbon of one of the conversation heart balloons in his fist. "Check this out."

Rose giggled. "Cute balloon, Trev."

"They're supposed to be like mistletoe. You kiss under them." He took two big steps and swept her into his arms. "Me, you, and this balloon, baby—the three of us are going to the sofa in the corner and staying there all night."

"God, I love you." She threw her arms around his neck as he shifted her higher on his chest like a bride.

His reply was muffled by her lips, but it sounded something like "*Gumph lumph yumph too*".

"Newlyweds." Lily sighed. "Too cute" Her mouth curved into a nostalgic smile as she gently shook her head.

I looked down at her to agree but stopped short. "Girl, just what in the heck are you wearing?"

She smoothed her hands down over the sides, then let them rest on her baby bump. "It's a Valentine's Day cardigan. Isn't it the cutest thing ever?"

My nose wrinkled up despite my hopeless quest to find something nice to say. "Yeah, I mean, it's something. I didn't know ugly Valentine's Day sweaters were a thing."

Her gasp was outraged. "It's not ugly! I'll have you know I made this myself."

"I'm sorry." My shoulders shrugged up. "Okay..."

It was bright red. There was fringe. And appliqued conversation hearts. Pastel sequins glittered in the dim overhead light of the storage room. It was hideous but I was not about to argue with someone who may be legally blind or at the very least in severe need of an appointment with an optometrist and a new pair of glasses.

"Well?" Her foot tapped on the floor.

"I love it. You, uh, made the hell out of that cardigan!"

"*Hmph,*" she scoffed. "Let's go out front, you can bring me a lemonade to make up for insulting my adorable sweater."

"You got it."

Chapter 4
This is how we brew it.

Liam

As usual, I was too early. My anxiety would never allow me to be late, or even on time. I sat in my car for a few minutes waiting but decided to head in and offer my help. I could see Violet bustling around in there by herself.

She had me retrieve a few wayward balloons and hang a banner outside, then sent me to a table with a cup of coffee. "You're the best. And I'm not humoring you, don't leave this table. Lily wants the best seat in the place so she can people watch, it's her thing. Don't let anybody snag it."

"Got it," I grinned. "Guard this table and drink your delicious coffee."

"Exactly. Thanks a latte, Liam. I appreciate you."

"Yeah," Jake chimed in as he strode through the swinging doors that led to the storage room. "You're teariffic, thanks for helping out." He looked to Violet, eyebrows up, for approval, but she shook her head.

"Nope." They shared a smile as he got closer. "Good try, baby, but we don't do tea here."

He dropped a kiss on her forehead. "Then I guess I can't tell you you're a hot-tea."

I sipped my coffee and tried not to listen, but it was impossible since they were standing at the edge of my table. It would have been awkward if it wasn't hovering on the border of hilarious. If you knew Violet even in passing, you knew coffee was her obsession and tea was her nemesis.

Her forehead crinkled as she thought it over. "I guess I'll allow it."

He winked at her. "I love you so matcha."

"And I love you a whole freakin' latte. But quit testing me."

"You know you love it, my beau-*tea*-ful Violet."

"Jake..." Her voice was breathy.

My eyes darted to my cup. "Well, obviously, you two were meant to bean." I said with a laugh, breaking the sexual tension I had unwittingly found myself in the middle of.

"I know, right?" A bemused smile crossed her face.

Jake winked at her, and she blushed, while I vowed never to be early to a party ever again. "I picked up the extra ice, gorgeous," he informed her. "I dumped it in the machine, okay?"

"Perfect. I guess it's time to get the par-tea started."

The door dinged with the first arrival, it was Luke.

Thank god for the interruption. I was about to be scarred for life.

"What the hell are you wearing, man?" I swear I was almost blinded by the sheer number of sequins glaring at me from his sweater. I was in a simple black suit, and he was in some sort of Valentine's Day monstrosity of a sweater. It looked like Cupid had pulled an all-nighter at a bar and then puked all over him.

"Lily made it for me. She has one too." He ran his hands down his chest, pulling a worried face when a piece of fringe snagged on his hand and tore off. "Look, it has my name on it." He pointed to a little yellow heart. "And this other one says, *Luke and Lily 4-Eva*". Isn't it great?"

"Okay, yeah it's nice." Great was not the word I would use, but he seemed happy about it, so I was too.

"She's been into crafts lately. Knitting, crocheting, sewing shit onto other shit, like this sweater." He shrugged and stuffed the fringe into one of the sweater's uneven pockets.

"I'm happy for you. I mean it." I wished the joy in his eyes was infectious because I wanted some of it for myself.

"All I wanted was to come home, you know? Get my old life back. Be with her again. I don't know if—" Emotion flashed across his face before he shook his head and looked away.

"What?" I was curious. For some reason, I had to know what he was thinking. I felt like he was a few steps ahead of me and I wanted to end up where he was someday.

"Sometimes I stop and wonder if this is real. Or just one of the old dreams I used to have."

"Hey, it's real," I reassured him. "We should talk about this with Jed next week." Luke's grandfather was a Vietnam veteran who ran a support group on his ranch. Luke and I attended it every week. Along with my therapist, the group helped me immeasurably. "Sometimes I feel the same way. I'll wake up and forget where I am."

"I'll bring it up. I don't ever want to go back to how I was."

"Same. I like it here."

He shot me a grin. "Me too."

"Hello, boys!" Dahlia, Holly's mom was headed our way. "Liam, I'm so happy you're here! I have someone for you to meet, she's right over there—" her hand waved behind her, gesturing to a pretty brunette standing by Violet's counter. Lucky for me she was facing the other way and didn't see me.

"Can we hold off on that for a second? I, uh, have to head to the restroom real quick." My chair squeaked as I stood, I threw out a hand to keep it from toppling over. "I'll be right back."

She sat at Luke's table and waved as I walked off. "Okay, honey. I'll be waiting for you right here."

And I'll be hiding in the back room for as long as humanly possible.

I did not want to be fixed up. I didn't want to meet anyone and lead them on. Currently, I had eyes for only one woman and until that changed, I did not want to date anyone else, it wouldn't be right.

I burst through the swinging doors. Maybe I could find a chair back here to wait it out on. Or maybe I'd go out the back door and ditch the party entirely.

"Liam!" Lily rushed over to me, followed by Holly. "Is everything okay? What are you doing back here?"

"Uh—"

"Is my mother out there?" Her hands hit her hips in outrage. "Is she trying to introduce you to someone—"

"Yeah," I stopped her. "I didn't let it get to the part where I found out her name. I told your mom I had to go to the restroom."

"Oh snap!" Lily patted my arm. Since she'd gotten back together with Luke, she had acted like a protective big sister toward me. It didn't seem to matter to her that I was actually a few years older. "That's good. Go hide out with Holly in Vi's office. Mom has got Jared Jamison all lined up for her."

"Okay—"

"Do not worry, both of you." She tapped her fist on her chest. "I got this. I'll just tell her you have diarrhea." Her head tilted in thought. "Maybe food poisoning would be better. What did you have for lunch? Whatever, it doesn't matter. Stomach issues will scare off whoever she wants you to meet. No one wants to dance with someone who has diarrhea or who could potentially barf at any moment. I'll think of something..." she muttered as she walked away.

"Wait—" Too late, she'd gone through the doors. I

turned to Holly. "Would she really tell everyone I have diarrhea?"

Her hand went to her mouth to stifle a giggle. "Oh yeah, she absolutely would."

"You think this is funny, do you?" My lips twitched in involuntary amusement.

"Hilarious," she confirmed with a guffaw. "But hey, it's better than the alternative, isn't it?"

"How so?"

"My mother is relentless, and you've successfully managed to dodge her first attempt at a setup. Way to go." She held up her hand for a high five.

Gamely, I gave it a light smack. "I guess there is a silver lining."

"For sure. And I have another one."

"Yeah?"

"Yep. Come with me." I followed her through Violet's office door. "Shut that," her whisper was equal parts adorable and conspiratorial. "We are not here."

"Ahh, got it." Softly, I closed the door behind myself. "Stealth mode."

"Exactly. I hid party snacks in the fridge when I was decorating earlier. Somehow, I knew I'd end up hiding out back here."

"You're a genius. Is there enough for two?"

"Of course." She laughed. "If there wasn't I'd make you go hide by yourself in the bathroom. Sit down, get comfy and I'll go get it."

I sat, settling into the cozy, flat surface that would be a perfect place to kiss her, lay her down, maybe peel that dress up over her sweet little body and get a taste of her, feel those sexy high heels dig into my back...

Damn it, stop.

"How long do you think we can get away with hiding back here?" I semi-shouted through the doorway while trying to get my rapidly spiraling thoughts back under control. I could hear the party starting out front. No one would hear me.

"That depends on Lily." Arms full, she re-entered the room with a wink. "And how bad your diarrhea is, of course." She set a couple of paper bags, a bottle of wine and two glasses on the coffee table in front of us then went to Violet's desk.

"Oh god." Mortified, I shook my head. "This is unreal." I liked this woman. A lot. I didn't have diarrhea but, like a curse, the word hovered in the air between us like the ultimate mood killer.

I had wanted to flirt with her, see if she was as interested in me as I was in her, but now I couldn't and maybe it was for the best because I shouldn't have these feelings for her in the first place—best friend's little sister-in-law and all that. It was easy to tell myself to stay away from her when I was alone, but every single time I got near her, my good decisions and best intentions went straight out the window and all I wanted to do was explore every possibility that came to me.

"Yes! Found it!" She turned to me, victoriously holding up a corkscrew. "Let's get comfortable. Take off your jacket. There's no way I'm dancing with Jared Jamison tonight—that's not gonna happen. I'm here in this office for the duration. Feel free to stay as long as you like, my mother can get real pushy and I am not in the mood." I slipped out of my suit jacket and tossed it to the chair in the corner where she had just placed her coat.

I had to stifle a groan when I saw what she was wearing. Tight and short were my two favorite things when it came to a dress and Holly's was both. She was stunning and suddenly I could think of nothing but what it would feel like to have those long, gorgeous legs of hers wrapped around my waist. And damn it, we were about to be alone in this office sitting on a plush, comfortable sofa. I was in so much trouble right now.

Think of the diarrhea...

I loosened my tie with a frustrated grimace. But I lost my frown when I noticed how avidly she watched as I undid the top two buttons of my dress shirt and began rolling the sleeves up. She bit her full, pink lower lip and I knew right then I had to be responsible and save us both before things got out of hand.

We had an undeniable chemistry between us, I felt it every time I was near her. But I had the sense she wasn't ready for it. And honestly, I wasn't either.

"What's in the bag, Holly?" I asked to break the spell she seemed to be under. Because If I joined her in that spell, we would absolutely end up naked.

"Huh?" she whispered with her hand at her throat. "Oh, right. The bags." Her head shook and she blinked rapidly. "Food. Snacks. Um, brie? Yeah, there's cheese and crackers. Uh, grapes?" As if it took great effort she focused on the bags and started unpacking them. "Tiny sandwiches cut into hearts. Cute, right?"

I nodded. Forget about the sandwiches, she was cute. I took in the sight of her pink cheeks and flustered demeanor, she was just as messed up over me as I was over her and I loved it even though it scared the shit out of me.

I grabbed the bottle of wine and corkscrew from the table. Why not add alcohol to the mix? That was always a smart choice.

My phone went off with a text notification. Then another one. And another one. This is how I knew it was Lily. She never texted once; it was always a series of messages.

Holly's laugh rang through the room. "Oh my god, that's Lily. She does that to you too? What did she say? Is it safe to go out front?"

LILY Stay back there.

LILY Mom has Liz McNaughton picked out for you.

LILY She's pretty and sweet but not right for you.

LILY Maybe she'd be good for Levi if he doesn't get his head out of his butt about Becca. What do you think?

LILY Never mind. Don't answer that. I can only focus on one thing at a time.

.   .   .

Holly's phone went off next. She laughed then flipped it around so I could read it.

CREEPY TWIN Jared Jamison left. He looked all sad.

CREEPY TWIN But that is not for you to worry about. YOU ARE NOT RESPONSIBLE FOR HIS CRUSH. Okay?

CREEPY TWIN Don't come out. Mom's still here and who knows who she'll try to get you to dance with now that he's gone.

CREEPY TWIN You're the last single sister and she has grandbaby fever. Like, what? The twins I'm carrying aren't enough for her?

CREEPY TWIN Oh Shit.

CREEPY TWIN She just read my text over my shoulder. DO NOT COME OUT HERE.

CREEPY TWIN I told her you're helping Liam with—you know…(the imaginary tummy troubles)

CREEPY TWIN Get him a snack from the fridge. I know you hid stuff in there. I AM ONTO YOU.

CREEPY TWIN Save me a cupcake. They're gone already.

CREEPY TWIN It's like, put pink sprinkles on something and people descend like vultures.

CREEPY TWIN I wanted a cupcake too, damn it.

Her eyes sparkled with humor. "She's a total nut and completely addicted to poop emojis and cupcakes."

"Agree. I've witnessed all of those things firsthand." I poured two glasses of wine and passed one to her.

"Thanks. Cheers to being single on Valentine's Day." Her voice was a velvet murmur, sexy and low.

Was she flirting with me or *was she just a natural sex bomb?* I couldn't tell yet.

"Here's to good company," I added benignly and clinked my glass to hers.

"That's sweet. Let's dig in, I'm starving. I haven't eaten all day and this cheese is calling my name."

"Cheese is my favorite food," I confessed. "Any kind. All of it."

"Oh my god, me too. I want to live in a house made of cheese, just like a little mouse." She sliced into the wheel of brie and offered me a piece.

"It's good to set clear goals. Or so I've heard." I joked before popping the brie into my mouth.

"Ahh, taking the piss. Love that. How do you like living in Luke's old house? I'm crashing with Jude and Levi, and I'd kill for my own space."

"I like it. It's just enough privacy without being lonely." Luke inherited his family's property, about thirty acres or so after his father passed. His old family home was at the back, and I rented it, while he, Lily, and their son lived in the new house at the front of the property.

"That sounds perfect. I was staying with my parents when I first got back to town, but my mother was driving me crazy. I love her, so much, but she can be overwhelming sometimes. We get along better when I'm not underfoot."

"I could see the need to be on your own. I get it."

"Yeah..." She let out a sigh and sipped her wine. "I think I need to figure out what I want to be when I grow up."

"No more blogging? I followed you for years."

"You did?" She sat straight and turned to face me, clearly surprised.

"Yeah, I did." No one knew I had followed her on social media, not even Luke. It came as a huge shock when I first saw her here in Sweetbriar. But for some reason, that I didn't yet understand, I had kept it to myself—until now.

Her travel blog and Instagram posts kept me going back when I was in Afghanistan. It wasn't anything other than her art that had drawn me to her back then, nothing like how I felt for her now. Her photos made me think of the home I had left behind. She had an eye for beauty and a true talent for photography. Plus, she was somewhat of an expert when it came to herbs and natural remedies, which had come in handy so many times over the years. I admired her expertise and the way she expressed herself through her words and images. Now I admired her for so much more than that.

"I missed home," she murmured. "I had a huge sense of wanderlust back when I blogged, but I don't anymore. I guess I got it out of my system because now I feel the opposite. I want to plant roots and grow them deep. I want my own place to make beautiful instead of finding the beauty in other places. Is that weird? I mean that I changed so much. It's practically opposite of what I was."

"I don't think it's weird at all. I want that too. I joined the Army so I could do more with my life, so I could help people, see new places, have new experiences and it was good—" a sardonic laugh escaped me. "Until it wasn't."

"Oh, Liam."

I didn't want my past to drag down this evening, so I shifted the subject back to her. "You could still blog. Just hiking up the mountain would provide tons of content. Locals know all the best spots."

"Yeah, but I'd be hated in town if I gave them all away, right?"

I chuckled. "Good point."

"Blogging isn't what it used to be anymore anyway. And that money has all run out. I need something steady. I'm not worried yet. It'll come to me." She held up a cracker with some kind of brown and black goop on it. "Here, taste this."

"I don't know, what is it?"

"It looks gross but trust me. Open."

I opened my mouth, and she placed the cracker

gently on my tongue. I hesitated before committing and she let out a cute giggle. Finally, I chewed and swallowed. "What was that?"

"Olive tapenade with herbs I picked from my mom's garden. Good, right?"

"You made that?"

"Yeah, don't get me wrong. I can't cook worth a damn, but I'm good at little things like this. My gram always said to have a few specialties up your sleeve to impress your party guests with."

"Well, I'm impressed. It looked like dog food, but I loved it."

My phone pinged again from the coffee table. Then again.

"Lily," we said in unison.

LILY ALL IS CLEAR ON THE WESTERN FRONT. That's a movie, right?

LILY Anyway. Liz went home, and my mother just left. Come out now. BRING ME CUPCAKES.

I flipped it around to show Holly. "I guess we should get back out there." I would much rather spend the rest of the night in this office getting to know her better.

"Back? Oh god, I never even went in at all. Violet's gonna be so mad."

"Nah, I wouldn't worry too much about that. She and Jake are on another level tonight. I think you'll be okay."

"That makes me feel a little bit better. Okay, I'll go out first. If they spot us together rumors will fly. You know how this town can be."

"Good thinking. I'll wait in here and clean up, then go."

"To the party. Not out the back door, right? We can be each other's buffer. I need a buffer, Liam. Please?"

"I won't leave." The thought of anyone hitting on her made me irrationally angry.

She reached out and touched my hand. "Thank you. I'll see you out there."

I watched her walk through the door with a sense of sadness. It felt like we had been in a bubble right here in this office and it had just popped.

Chapter 5
I have coffee-lings for you.

Holly

Oh, damn, damn, damn. I was in for it.

There were too many things about him to like now. The obvious basics, like his looks, and what had to be an ingrained hot guy ability to roll up his dress sleeves and make it sexy—arm porn! *Gah!* His hair had grown out since moving to town. No more military buzzcut, now he had thick, dark brown waves that sometimes flopped onto his forehead. It had been so hard to keep myself from reaching out to push it back. It was so gorgeous, just like the entire tall, muscled, and sexy rest of him.

But what pushed it over the top was just *him*. He had hidden depths that I wanted to explore. He had a still, soft aura that felt warm and comforting and I didn't want to leave the office. But I had to.

I wasn't ready for anything deeper than a Valentine's

Day conversation. I had come here wanting to kiss him, to have fun. But he would be more than fun if I let him in any more than I already had.

I hesitated at the swinging doors to the front of the store. I heard the laughter and fun of the party and it felt like another world existed in there and I wanted to go back to the one I had discovered in Vi's office with Liam.

"Oh well," I muttered. I was used to letting good things pass me by. This was just one more.

I jumped as the door hit my arm. It was Violet. "Holly. Oh my god, take these balloons." She shoved the strings from the conversation heart balloons in my hands. "I made a mistake. Valentine's Day is nothing like Christmas. People are horny and lonely on Valentine's Day; you were so right. These balloons have unleashed a horndog apocalypse into my shop. It's like one of those basement parties back in high school. And Trevor and Rose are the worst! They haven't come up for air, not even once!"

I hid a laugh. "I'm so sorry your party is ruined."

Someone called her name with a question I could barely hear and she turned. "No, you may not use my office for a quickie. Show some decorum, Mrs. Robinson. You are a mother and a teacher!" She turned back to me again. "Oh my god! Will you please stay back here? Guard the back room, don't let anyone get in here. Thank god Liam is still in the bathroom. How is his tummy trouble anyway? Tell him I have Tums on my desk—" She turned back to the party. "Lily!" she shrieked. "Erase the chalkboard out front." She grabbed my shoulders. "No more balloons, pop them all! People are hooking up in their cars, Holly. The parking lot is no longer safe for children. What have I done? I have to get back out there."

"Uh, good luck."

The door swung shut and I felt him approach. I knew he was there. Behind me, beneath the balloons.

I turned around and our eyes locked before he lifted his to the balloons held tight in my grip. He knew what they were supposed to mean, and I did too. They felt like permission. A dozen or so balloons telling me that yes, it was indeed a great idea to make out with Liam in the back room.

He reached out and touched my wrist, one tiny touch, before letting his hand drop to his side.

My heartbeat immediately rushed to the spot. It was only my wrist, but it burned, imprinting the memory of how it felt to have his hand on me, even in such an innocent place as my wrist.

A shiver passed through me when he smiled, soft and sweet. It was a smile just for me, I could tell by the way his eyes locked to mine and his body bowed forward.

He studied my face with those gorgeous intense brown eyes of his and my body turned liquid under his perusal. If he were looking for a sign of objection, he wasn't going to find it. I watched in anticipation as his tongue darted out to wet his lower lip.

I knew he wanted to kiss me, and I was going to let him.

I nodded, almost imperceptibly, because I didn't want to admit, especially to myself, how much I wanted to know how it would feel to have his mouth on mine.

His smile faded and he bit his lip, face lowering inch by inch as I leaned into his warmth to place a hand on his broad wall of a chest—*for balance,* I lied to myself.

My heart took a perilous leap in my chest, then rushed out of control when he threaded his fingers through my hair and tugged me gently within his reach. This caress was a command, gentle but demanding and I was here for it.

"Yes," I whispered without sound, and he nodded.

Slowly, seductively, his gaze drifted to my parted lips, they tingled like he was already kissing me.

I burned. My god, I could feel him everywhere.

I let my eyes drift closed. I'd given my permission and now it was up to him to decide.

"This is it." His voice was a deep growl, I felt it like a touch.

"Do it," I whispered. "Kiss me."

After a sharp inhale, his thumb went to my jaw to keep my face steady with his huge warm palm. "My god, you're so fucking beautiful."

I couldn't answer, I had no words in my head other than a soft breathy moan that sounded kind of like "*yes*" as he backed me into the wall by the swinging door. Balloons flew to the ceiling; their ribbons tickled the sides of my face as I let them go to clutch his shirt tight with both of my fists. There was no way I would let him stop now. I had never experienced anything like this, I had to find out where it would lead.

His stubbled chin grazed my cheek as he slid his nose along mine, breathing me in before his mouth hungrily covered my lips. Urgent, exploratory, and reckless, we got to know each other better.

It was almost too much. It felt too good, like nothing I'd felt before, ever. It was everything I didn't know I needed, and it went straight to my head, turning me into a trembling mess of sensation in his arms.

He pulled away with a gasp. "Holly, are you sure about this?"

"No, but don't stop, I want more," I demanded.

He kissed me again like a whisper and I returned it with crazed abandon, thrusting my tongue between his parted lips with a groan as he crushed me to him, his insistent hands at my waist sliding lower until his finger-tips dug into the top of my ass and his leg slid between mine.

"Holly, what are we doing?" He whispered, his breath hot against my ear.

"I have no idea, but I'm not ready for it to end yet." I tucked my face into his throat, kissing the steady pulse at the base as he held me tight.

We couldn't seem to stop, instinct kept drawing us closer each time we managed to break apart.

He pulled away again, but still held me gently as his hands loosened their grip on my waist and he moved them up to brush my hair over my shoulders. I ached to be closer, I didn't want to let him go. Something tangible existed between us now, small threads of feelings had knit themselves into something strong, something I could no longer shove out of my mind and deny. My heart lurched in my chest, wanting to be close to his again.

He looked at me lazily, through half-closed lids before blinking as if in shock. I watched as his emotions played over his face and I knew he felt it too.

I was left speechless, breathless, and completely lost in the solid strength of his arms. I didn't want this feeling to end. I didn't want to let go.

I was in trouble.

I wasn't ready to feel this way. But there was nothing I could do to stop the waves of tenderness from washing over me. I couldn't fight the desire in my heart to pull him close and not let go.

This was pure chemistry. The kind that exploded and sent people reeling. Made them make rash choices and foolish declarations. The kind that could break hearts if one wasn't careful. We were like a damn nuclear bomb about to explode.

"I knew it," he whispered.

"Knew what?" I breathed.

"That you would change everything."

"Liam..." I whispered. He was right. Nothing would be the same for us. Not after this.

Get more Liam and Holly in Heart to Heart!
Available Now!
Want to get to know Luke better?
Meet him in In My Heart, out now!

In My Heart

Luke was my first love, my first kiss, my first everything. He always swore I was his reason to live but he lost himself in the army then I lost him.

I never thought I could be with anyone after him, but I was.

I never thought I'd go back to the small town where we grew up, but I did.

Running back to my family as a thirty-year-old widow was never in my life plan. But for the sake of my children I returned home to the memories I had fought so hard to leave behind.

What I didn't know was that Luke was back too. With only one thing on his mind. Me.

But there is something he doesn't know and our son can't wait to tell him what he's missed.

Our past brought us back together but if we can't trust each other it will tear us apart.

Available Now!

Chapter 1

Luke

One more swing and the tree fell. The scent of dirt blasting into the air filled my lungs while the sunlight filtering through the pines cast the forest floor in spiky patterns of shadow and light. I let my senses fill, grounding myself against the regrets threatening to derail the progress I had made since returning home from Afghanistan.

I was a father.

I had a son. If I got a handle on myself, I might be able to meet him and see his mother again. My Lily was also back in Sweetbriar, our small Oregon hometown. The thought of seeing her again after everything I had done and how I had ended it all—

I cut Lily out of my life. I had thought she deserved so much more than what I could offer. After a certain point, the things I'd seen and done in the Army had blended together into a black cloud of hurt and pain and I could no longer process what was happening to me. My grandfather tried to help but you can't help someone who feels worthless, so I cut him out too and stayed away from Sweetbriar.

Frustrated, I wiped the back of my hand across my sweaty brow, then took swing after swing at the fallen tree, splitting it into manageable pieces. Some of it I would use for firewood; the rest I would carve into animals, or chess pieces, or paperweights, or whatever else crossed through my thoughts the next time I needed to disconnect from the world.

My muscles burned and my still-injured back ached as I straightened but pain wasn't enough to make me forget what I had done. Nothing ever was. I could never disconnect from Lily. She was branded on my soul. No matter how far apart we were or how many years went by, she was always there. Memories played on a loop in my mind like an old black and white movie—sometimes skipping, sometimes blurry, but never gone. Those memories pulled me through some of the worst moments of my life, even when I had wanted so badly to let go of everything and fade away.

When I found out she was coming home my life burst back into color. Everywhere I went in this town held a moment we shared. She was on my mind constantly and it was driving me to distraction. It hurt. The desperate yearning in my chest grew bigger every day, overwhelming all other facets of my world until all I could think of was how to convince her to let me back into her life again.

I wondered how she was now. My heart broke for her when I found out her husband died. Then I was sick at myself for being happy I might have a shot to get her back. And my son? I wanted him too. I wanted my life to be the way it should have been before I fucked it all up.

All these years, I had told myself I'd done the right thing. But now that I was home and finally healing, I knew letting her go was the worst mistake of my life.

After my medical discharge from the Army, I was a disaster. My grandfather Jed, or Pops as I had always called him, a Vietnam vet, convinced me to get help. I was diagnosed with PTSD, which should have been obvious to me, but it hadn't been. Denial is a powerful tool when your only goal is to forget. Pops took me to his therapist, talked me through panic attacks, comforted me when I realized all that I had thrown away, then gave me Rocky, my sort-of emotional support dog. Rocky had failed out of Jed's ESD program, but I fell in love with the brown and white boxer when he refused to leave my side. He woke me from nightmares, nudged me whenever I got down on myself, and provided me with the kind of love only the best, most loyal dogs could. Rocky was currently dozing off under a tree.

Pops and his employees trained service dogs of all kinds on his ranch right outside of Sweetbriar. I stayed with him for about a month before moving back to the house where I grew up. And it must be said, there is something about being surrounded by puppies and wide-open spaces that could put anyone at ease. It was the perfect way to begin settling back into a normal life.

I inherited my childhood home after my father passed. He'd made quite a few changes to the house while I was in the Army, to the point it almost felt like a different place. But the land was the same—fifty acres that backed into the Cascade Mountains in Oregon. I had since readjusted to the quiet sounds that had been so familiar in my childhood: animals rustling through the brush, the rush of the river, wind blowing through the trees. After being surrounded by people and near constant activity it was difficult at first, but I finally realized getting acclimated to peace and solitude was a blessing.

"Yo, McCabe!" My former sergeant, Liam, called to me from the trees. He was my brother, bonded irrevocably not by the blood that flowed through our veins but by the blood we had lost together over the last few years.

Rocky's ears pricked up, but he didn't budge; by now he knew Liam almost as well as he knew me.

"Hey." I took another swing and left the axe in the wood. "How was work?"

"Typical. Boring. Quiet." He grinned at me. "Small town life is exactly what I needed."

"I grew up here. It's not always boring and quiet, you know." Like any small town, Sweetbriar had its fair share of gossip and low-key intrigue.

His lips tipped up in a grin. "Duly noted. How was therapy?" I was glad to see him smile. I wasn't the only one who was a mess when we got here.

"The physical stuff is always easier. Talking about myself was never my thing." Liam and I served together, we were both medically discharged due to the same IED attack. I convinced him to come with me to Sweetbriar and help me run my late father's construction company.

"Swinging that axe can't be good for your back," he remarked.

I shrugged. "As long as I do it right, I'm fine."

He smirked. "You're full of shit."

"I needed to—" I ran a hand down my face, unsure of what I was trying to say. But Liam knew.

"You needed to get it out. The way you feel about her being here . . . it's real now. No more *if* or *when*. They're both in town and it's just a matter of time before you see them."

"I'm nervous as fuck," I admitted.

"I can't blame you for that. You've been building this up in your mind for a long time."

"It's everything, man. If I screw this up, what do I have?"

"Hey, look. For one, that's not going to happen. And two, both of us know by now it's not healthy to think that way. We have each other, and Jed, and my grandmother. Neither one of us is alone."

"Is that your therapist or mine talking?" I joked. The mood out here had gotten too serious for my liking.

"Hard to tell lately, but that doesn't make it not true." He passed me a bottled water before sitting by Rocky beneath the tree and scratching him behind his ears.

"You're right." I sighed.

"Let's go get coffee. That's what I came out here for." He chuckled.

"Good idea." Lily's sister, Violet, owned the only coffee shop worth going to in town. If I got lucky, maybe I'd run into Lily there. Last time I spoke to Violet, she had mentioned hiring Lily for the summer.

"Call Jed, have him meet us."

"The old man texts now. I taught him how to use his smart phone. The memes are endless."

He huffed a laugh. "Let's go."

I shot Pops a text, Liam woke Rocky, then we took off. Liam drove, just like he always had when we were deployed.

"Pops is busy. Just you and me this time."

He nodded his answer as he took us out of the mountains and down into town. I lowered the window in back for Rocky and cranked the air conditioner up high for me and Liam. It was an unusually hot summer day in Sweetbriar and, since returning from Afghanistan, we were all about creature comforts. Air conditioning, warm blankets, endless hot showers, and sleeping in. Don't get me started on hot coffee and good food. Violet got my business more than once a day, and I'll leave it at that.

We also set our own hours at my father's—well, now *my* company, McCabe Construction. Dad had built it to unbelievable levels while I was gone. I'd inherited enough money that I never had to work again if I chose not to. But I couldn't sell the business and leave his employees jobless. Plus, I needed something to do, so I stayed and gave them all raises, just to spite my father's cheap ass ghost in case it was lurking around somewhere, still disapproving of my choices.

He pulled into Violet's parking lot and cut the engine.

"There's my guys!" Violet greeted us from her perch behind the counter. She was older than me by a few years and I'd known her my whole life. She'd always been like an older sister to me. "The usual?"

"Please," Liam affirmed with a huge smile while I hung back and nodded. It was after lunchtime, and her shop was always slower this time of day. We practically had the place to ourselves. She turned her back to prepare our orders and I contemplated how to get her to start talking about Lily without having to ask.

She slid our coffees and a plate of scones across the counter. "Lily won't be in town until tomorrow. She was up all night with Calla. The poor little thing is cutting a tooth." Calla was Lily's baby, about six months old.

"Thanks, Violet." Liam paid for our orders and headed to the sofa in the back corner of the shop. I let Rocky follow him.

I took my drink with a sheepish smile. "Uh, I was going—"

She reached out and patted my arm with a knowing grin on her face. "And now you don't have to ask me about her. You're welcome."

"Thank you, Vi. You've made this easy on me, and I appreciate it."

"Well, I'm glad you're finally home. You and Lily belong together. You always have."

"I didn't realize how much I missed her in my life until I got back and got my head on straight. She's essential—I can't be myself without her."

Her eyes melted as she gave me a smile. "I love the way you talk about her."

I pressed my lips together and studied my shoes, embarrassed. What if Lily wouldn't talk to me? I'd end up a lovesick idiot with his unrequited feelings on display for an entire town to ridicule.

"Hey, it's okay." Her smile grew sympathetic. "Your face shows your love, Luke. It's in your body language and the words you choose when you talk about her. You have always loved her, ever since you were little kids. Once she sees you and hears you out, that simple fact will sink in."

"I hope you're right. But I'm not going to rush anything. We started off as friends, and I have to be okay with it if that's all she wants."

"I know. But if ever any two people belonged together, it's the two of you."

"Well, I can't imagine not having her back in my life. She's been in my heart forever, Violet. I never let her go."

"None of us let you go either. You're part of the family, Luke."

Violet gave me a nod and turned around to tidy behind the counter. I joined Liam and kept trying to come up with a way to get close to Lily again.

Heart Words

The last person I wanted to see was the hot jerk who
broke my heart.
Unfortunately, his daughter is the newest and most
adorable kindergartner in my class, and he is the newest,
hottest, and most annoyingly determined cop in town.

Falling for Trevor again was not part of my plan.
Burying my feelings, avoiding him at all costs, and
keeping him out of my heart. That was the plan.

But this flame flickering between us refuses to die and he
still seems to be everything I've ever wanted. Protective,
sexy, and kind, and that doesn't even get into how I feel
when I see him with his kids.

He asked me for a second chance. But how can I take it
when it feels like we never really took the first one?

Available Now!

Chapter 1

Rose

I sipped my hazelnut latte and smiled gratefully at my older sister. Violet always gave good coffee. Sometimes she also provided unwanted advice and nosy observations, but I decided to ignore those and focus on the positive aspects of having her as a volunteer in my classroom. If the first day of school was hectic, then the first day of kindergarten was utter insanity. Nervous children barely out of toddlerhood combined with teary-eyed, emotional parents made for an intense morning. Volunteers were necessary. Volunteers who provided coffee were invaluable.

"Are you ready, Violet?" I asked after taking another sip.

"Yep. But the real question is, are you ready?" She peered at me over the top of her coffee cup, eyebrows standing at attention and hazel eyes twinkling. She expected the scoop, but I wasn't ready to give it up. "Madison is going to be in your class this year, which means Trevor will be here any minute to drop her off." Madison was the adorable daughter of my—well, he wasn't even my ex. Trevor was my almost. He'd never fully owned my heart, yet he'd broken it all the same.

Trevor Hale was the delicious new detective on my police chief-father's force. I wanted him from the second I saw him over a year ago, standing in my sister's living room looking gorgeous and irresistible. For a while, he wanted me too. But it didn't last. Nothing ever lasts for me, because something about me was forgettable. Easily-replaceable Rose. Well, no more of that. I had made a sacred vow to myself to find a man who wanted me as much as I wanted him. No more complicated, messy relationships and no more settling for second place.

"Earth to Rose . . ." Violet teased.

I took another sip of my latte and smiled at her. "I'm ready. You know, the first day of school is always my favorite." She looked at me skeptically as I smoothed down my navy blue, red apple-printed shirt-waist dress. I tapped my red T-strap flats on the floor, and flashed my matching red manicure at her, making her laugh. I could go over the top with my school attire. My goal in life ever since I was a child was to be just like Ms. Frizzle from *The Magic School Bus*. She always wore dresses inspired by her lessons and made learning fun. Seeing a child become inspired in my classroom meant everything to me. I refused to allow the thought of seeing Trevor this morning throw me for a loop. This was my world, and I had important work to do.

"We have about ten minutes 'til game time. Just enough time for you to spill about what went on between you and Trevor," she said as she sipped her coffee and walked the room, making sure everything was in its place. Every year, Violet helped me set up my classroom. This year we decorated with a black chalkboard and neon rainbow theme. Violet owned a hugely successful coffee shop in town called *Violet's*. But before becoming the coffee guru of Sweetbriar, Oregon, she was an educational assistant. She kept herself on the volunteer list and usually spent the first week or two of school with me. Kindergarteners were like kittens for the first few weeks; all hyper and easily distracted. Herding cats was a multi-person job.

"Nothing happened," I lied as I checked my makeup in the mirror hanging behind my desk. After fluffing my long, curly red hair, I applied more lip gloss. I wasn't usually a primper, but I was nervous as all heck. The closer it got to start time, the more fidgety I became. I didn't usually get nervous on the first day of school. In fact, my classroom was the only place that I felt confident. Every other aspect of my life was kind of a disaster. And now, because of Trevor and our almost-thing together, I was pretty much a nervous wreck in the one place that made me feel good about myself.

Damn it, Sexy Trevor. Get out of my brain.

"Oh, come on. You met him at Lily's, right? And then you had a secret affair with him. Is that it? Did he move here to be with you? Come on, I won't tell anyone!" She waggled her eyebrows at me. Lily was our sister, and my identical twin. Trevor was her late husband's partner on the police force. I did meet him at her old house; Violet was half right.

"I don't want to talk about this Violet. Now is not the time," I insisted as I continued with my excessive primping.

Violet's voice greeting a student snapped me out of my vain reverie. Whipping around, I hastily stashed my lip gloss in my desk and hurried to join her at the door to say hello to the little early bird. I'd met most of the students at back to school night last week, but not this little cutie.

"Good morning. My name is Miss Barrett. What's your name?"

"I'm Anna," she answered distractedly as she stared at me. "Your hair is just like Merida's. From *Brave*. She's my favorite princess." I tried my best to tame my curls, but they had a mind of their own. I kept my hair long because the longer it was, the easier it was to take care of. The weight of it hanging down my back kept me from looking like a frizzy red Q-tip.

"Well, thank you. I like that movie too." I looked up from cute little Anna and shook Anna's mother's hand. "Would you like to go to your table and write your name on the paper, then match it to your name on the wall and put it in the slot?" Anna looked intrigued. All the tables had a label with each student's name, blank slips of paper, and baskets full of crayons. Violet called them over to Anna's table.

The second she turned from me to go to her table, Trevor popped right back into my brain just like a freaking whack-a-mole. I'd like to whack him out of my mind, but ever since I'd seen him at my mom's Sunday dinner with Lily and the kids, I couldn't get him out of my thoughts. That day, I'd taken one look at him, turned around and rushed out of the house. I have been actively avoiding him ever since. He hadn't attended back-to-school night with his kids; his mother had brought them, which was a relief at the time. But now, I wished I'd seen him and gotten it over with. The anticipation was killing me.

My younger brother Jude came through the door next, which distracted me enough to allow me to whack Trevor back into his hole in my brain. Jude was with Bella, the daughter of one of his good friends. Poor Harper had to work this morning and couldn't bring Bella herself. Little Bella was crying and Jude was doing his best to console her, but it wasn't working. "I'm trying, Rose, but she just wants Harper."

I bent down to talk to her. "Hi, Bella. You remember me and Violet, right?" She nodded through her tears. "Yay! Do you remember that we're both super nice, and extra awesome?" I teased with a big smile. She looked up at me and returned a tiny smile. "You'll be fine today. I know that your mom is going to pick you up right after school, and you can tell her all about how much fun you had on your first day of kindergarten." She took a deep breath and nodded. Violet waved her over to her table. Jude mouthed 'thank you' to me, then followed them.

It went on from there. Kids arrived, Violet and I gave greetings and introductions, the little tables filled up—but there was no sign of Trevor. I was a jumble of nerves. I just wanted to get the part where I had to see him over with, so I could go on with my day.

I heard him before I saw him. His voice was a trigger, popping him back up to fill my thoughts. Only this time, all the memories popped up too. Trevor and I had been long distance. We'd built most of our relationship over the phone—as in every night before bed, plus here and there throughout our days—for a little over three months. We'd never even kissed, and sadly, it was the best relationship I'd ever had. What did that say about me? *Pathetic, that's what it said.*

Violet bustled around the room, talking to parents and helping kids write their names. I had to suck it up. Tamping down my feelings, I headed to the door to greet Madison and Trevor. "Hi, Madison. Are you excited for your first day of kindergarten?" I asked with a big, partially-fake smile.

I briefly glanced up at Trevor and he smiled at me. Damn, he looked edible—tall with strong, lean muscles on glorious display in the black polo shirt that stretched over his broad chest. His brown eyes twinkled at me and that gorgeous smile weakened my resolve to never speak to him again.

I shook my head slightly. *Quit it, Rose, you're at work, look away.*

I refocused on Madison, who clung to Trevor's hand with fear on her face and a trembling chin. As her big blue eyes filled with tears, I forgot all about Trevor and lost my nervous jitters.

I knelt in front of her. "We're going to have a great day, Madison. We'll sing songs and color pictures. We'll play outside and go for a walk around the school so you will know where everything is. I promise to teach you everything you need to know about being a kindergartner. Then you can go home and tell your dad all about it. Deal?" I held my hand out to her, and she shook it with a shy smile. *Yes!*

I stood up, slipping a bit on the carpet. Trevor held my elbow to steady me.

"Thank you," I whispered, as the electricity from his touch zoomed through my body. *Damn it, no sexy electricity allowed!* Trevor was like catnip, and I was the stupid cat.

"You're welcome, Rosalie." he said, not letting me go. He studied my face while I squirmed under his observation. I guess I hadn't tamped my feelings down far enough. Who was I kidding? I had so many unresolved feelings for Trevor that I'd have to turn my heart into a landfill to bury them all.

Violet called to Madison and waved to her from her table. She looked up at Trevor, who nodded encouragingly. Madison headed over to Violet and sat down.

"You haven't been taking my calls," he said softly, once she was out of earshot. No way I was taking his calls. Trevor was irresistible over the phone. His deep, smoky voice did things to me—things that were too inappropriate to be thinking about here.

I sighed, frustrated and confused by my lingering feelings for him. "I've been busy. Getting ready for the school year to start. I'm sorry," I murmured.

"If I call you tonight, will you answer?" I shook my head as his deep voice washed over me and I shivered. Damn him and his hotness. "I know I hurt you. It hurt me too, Rose. But we could have another chance together. Please? Can we try again?" he whispered intently. Gorgeous eyes burned into mine, drawing me in. I had to look away from that eyeball tractor beam, lest I end up headfirst in the garbage again.

"I can't do this right now." He looked like he wanted to argue. "You can call me tomorrow night," I said, simply to placate him and get him to go away so I could attempt to have a normal day.

"Okay, tomorrow then. I'm going to say goodbye to Madison." Violet had switched name tags and moved her to sit by an also-crying Bella. Over the years, I had found that when you put two crying little girls together, they always ended up as friends. I shot Violet a thumbs up.

I pulled myself together. I had until tomorrow night to come up with something to say to him. Trying to avoid him wasn't going to work anymore. It was clear he would not be giving up any time soon. Madison beamed up at him as he tugged one of her pigtails, straightening the corkscrew curl. And he just got hotter.

From the Heart

I was his one who got away, or so he said.

Falling for Jake was not part of my plan. I should have stuck to rebuilding my life as a divorcee.

My ex-husband's irresistible best friend was the last kind of complication I needed at this point in my life even though he was the one I saw first all those years ago.

Being with Jake was a risk I was afraid to take but I couldn't resist him and he knew it.

And after spending years with the wrong man, I finally feel wanted, beautiful, adored.

But now things are even more tangled because our one accidental night together has me unexpectedly expecting.

Will he be the one to stay?
Or become my one who got away?

Available Now!

Chapter 1

Violet

"I don't have enough coffee or middle fingers for today."

E verything that could possibly go wrong in a day had already gone wrong and the clock had yet to strike eight a.m. I woke up confused and cranky well after my alarm had gone off and after finally making it outside to leave for work, I was greeted by a flat tire. It only spiraled further down the crapper from there.

Currently, I was back at home sitting in my car with my head pounding from what was sure to become a migraine. I was also covered in almost dry, sticky foam courtesy of my hell-bent-on-betrayal espresso machine and some unruly steamed milk. But I had known something was about to go extra-horrid-change-your-life-wrong the second I had approached my driveway and saw my husband's latest Porsche still parked in the driveway—with his secretary's little red Honda parked next to it. Apparently, my coffee shop's espresso machine wasn't the only thing in the mood to stab me in the back this morning.

I pulled in behind the Honda, shut off the engine and stormed out of my car. All I wanted was a shower, some fricking Advil, and maybe a damn nap. It looked like I was going to get a whole lot more than that. I was about to see something horrible. I could feel it.

How do you know when a marriage is over?

Several times over the years, I'd tried to recall the moment—or even a ballpark time period—when my marriage went from happy to . . . less happy. From shaky to in serious trouble. But I could never do it. Tom and I had loved each other once; that was a fact. But somewhere along the way, we'd grown apart. Hence why I'd made the choice to soon file for divorce. I had decided that February first would be the day to tell our sons. I didn't want to taint the holiday season for them.

A wave of nausea hit me as I approached the porch and the *snick* of my key in the lock made me flinch, but I persevered and stepped into the foyer anyway. After deciding to head up the back stairs, I tossed my keys on the kitchen island and tried to mentally prepare for whatever I was about to discover.

Choking back bile, I started up the stairs. I didn't want to catch him in the act, yet I couldn't force myself to turn around and leave. The car in the driveway was my first clue—of today, at least. The knock-off Louis Vuitton bag I spied sitting on the stairs was the second.

I continued down the hall to our bedroom. Tom and I had moved into this house almost twelve years ago. The same year our twin boys started kindergarten and I opened my coffee shop in town. My pregnancy had been a surprise, but Tom had insisted it was meant to be. After we got married, I left college to have the boys and found a job as an educational assistant. Tom had been in his junior year and gone on to graduate, then worked his way up to owning his own real estate agency right here in Sweetbriar, Oregon. He was ambitious and determined to make a good life for us, and he did it. But he had developed expensive taste over the years and the more money he made, the more his sweet disposition had disappeared. Sadly, he replaced it with a big-ass ego, an air of condescension, and an overabundance of concern about what other people thought of him. Keeping up with the Joneses was not good enough for Tom. He preferred to lord his success over everyone we knew. He wanted to be the only Jones in town.

A finite number of happy family smiles greeted me as I passed the portraits and school pictures lining the hallway. I ended up standing in front of our wedding photo, hung in an inset arch, right next to our bedroom door.

Who was that girl?

Hope shone in her eyes while two baby boys grew in her belly. Tom had worn a rented tuxedo and an adorable, sweet smile that I hadn't seen in far too many years to count.

"Tom! Tom! Tommy!" a woman moaned. It sounded like his secretary. I kept forgetting her name. Or maybe I had just subconsciously refused to remember it. It had been clear upon meeting her that her goal was to end up right here—beneath my snake-in-the-grass husband.

"Bethany, baby—" he grunted.

Bethany. That's it.

Through the partially open door, I could hear the rhythmic squeak of the box spring and the slap of his hips against hers.

Cheating on me in my own damn house.

As if in a trance, I pushed the door all the way open to see them, naked, right in the middle of the bed. They faced the mirror over the dresser, too wrapped up in the obscene show they were putting on for themselves to notice they had an audience.

"Tommy. Please. Please. Please," she begged as she writhed beneath him.

He collapsed forward onto her back, kissed her neck, and said, "I love you, babydoll."

My stomach twisted into a knot as time stood still. I let out a gasp, and suddenly trying to recall the precise day things started to change between us didn't matter anymore. My marriage was now officially over.

February first could eff right off. No one cheats on me.

He rose to his knees when he heard me gasp. "Violet! Shit!"

We locked eyes for one brief moment until he scrambled for his robe at the foot of the bed and put it on. Almost eighteen years of marriage and all he had to say was *"Violet! Shit!"*?

"What are you doing here?" He looked annoyed.

"Excuse me?" I wasn't the one banging someone else in our freaking marital bed on my brand-new sheets. "Uh, I live here, and I have a headache." Maybe I should leave. But I still couldn't make myself move. My marriage had gone up in flames. But here I stood, allowing myself to feel the burn.

"Another headache? Really?" he scoffed.

"Oops," Bethany chimed in with a satisfied smirk on her face. She rose to her knees next to Tom, then snatched his T-shirt from the edge of the bed to put on. "Maybe I'll let you two talk for a few minutes. Do you need to talk to her, honey?" *Yuck*, baby talk. And, who in the heck does this girl think she is?

"Yes. I do." He nodded as his eyes darted swiftly between the two of us. Caught between past and present. Wife and mistress.

She kissed his neck and smirked at me when he sucked in a breath. "Don't forget who you belong to now," she whispered as she got up to saunter into my bathroom.

Would fire be enough to get skank off my towels?

Despite all my instincts telling me to get the hell out of there, I stood still with my temper simmering beneath the surface. It pushed all other feelings to the back burner, and I was grateful for it.

After a nervous sigh, he finally addressed me. "Violet, have you checked your email today? You always check it first thing in the morning. Don't let your *headaches* start affecting how you run your business—"

"What? Email? No. My morning has been a total disaster." Each word he said fueled my anger but, like usual, something held me back from expressing it. Later, I was sure there would be other feelings—humiliation, grief for the loss of the family I had fought so hard to keep, possibly nostalgia, and maybe worry for my boys and our future. But for now, rage was working for me. It kept me on my feet, and I needed to stay upright so I could leave with my dignity intact.

He drove a hand into his hair and let out a huff. "I explained everything in the email. You shouldn't be here right now. I didn't intend for you to see this. But now that you've just seen me with Bethany you should know that we're in love, Vi. And this isn't just an affair, or a fling. I want a divorce so I can marry her. I thought maybe you could pack your stuff this weekend—"

"Are you crazy?" He'd gone crazy. Absolutely, totally insane. "*You* pack your stuff this weekend. I'm not leaving my house," I argued, because what the hell? We had sons together. This was our *family's* house.

"We wouldn't have this house if it weren't for me. You can't afford to keep this place on your own, and you know it. The boys can stay with me until you find your own place."

I was not about to leave my boys with him and his new *girlfriend*. I panicked and swiftly changed course. My sons were more important to me than staying in this house. "I guess you've got it all figured out. Fine, I'll leave. But I'm taking the boys with me. And this argument isn't over."

"Obviously, it's not over. We'll need to file for divorce," he huffed indignantly. "Fine, great. You're right, they should be with you. I'm taking Bethany up the mountain to ski for the weekend anyway—which I also told you about in the email—so you can pack up your stuff and a few things for the boys while I'm gone."

"Skiing? I thought you had a real-estate conference in Portland." My face fell. *I am so stupid.*

He shook his head. "I really didn't want you to find out like this . . ." The statement hung in the air as if there were nothing else to say.

"So you sent an email? A freaking email—*Gah!* You are unbelievable know we were having problems, but to end it this way? After all these years together? Cheating on me? And a fucking email? You couldn't have just sat down and talked to me and asked for a divorce like a decent person?"

His head dropped. "Vi, I don't know what to say."

"Oh, I don't know—you could try *I'm sorry*?" *Motherfucker.*

Morbid curiosity kept me asking questions I didn't really want the answers to. "How long has this been going on?" I demanded.

His eyes darted to the bathroom door. "Physically? A little over six months."

Physically.

"Six months," I repeated on a breath. It had been almost a year since we had been intimate. Plus, two years of marriage counseling that clearly didn't take. Too much time and money had been spent on dates and dinners with my husband that, according to our marriage counselor, would put the fire back into our marriage. But I had been wasting my time trying to rekindle what had already been a pile of ash.

I looked to the floor with thoughts of STDs and tiny little Toms running around Sweetbriar darting through my mind. "Are there more? I mean, other than Bethany?" The fact that I hadn't lost my shit yet was astonishing. Either I was stronger than I thought, or it would all come out later in some kind of epic lady-tantrum. Hopefully, I would be alone whenever it occurred.

Earnest eyes met mine and for a brief second and I recognized the man I used to know. "No! Just her. I swear, Vi. It's only ever been Bethany." I studied his face with narrowed eyes. I believed him. But I would make a doctor's appointment anyway, just in case. I'd obviously been wrong about him before.

I needed to get out of here. After spinning on my heel, I crossed the hallway to the stairs to leave.

Sudden realization halted my progress, and I froze at the top of the stairs with a bitter laugh. All my plans revolved around stupid, freaking February first. My sister Rose had just gotten married on New Year's Eve and I'd been planning to buy her house and move in with my boys. But not yet, dammit! I needed more time to figure out what to say to them, and she needed to finish moving her stuff out. *Crap!*

My bed was tainted. I could never sleep in it again. This whole house was dirty with betrayal and filled up with lies. The filth would be impossible to scrub away. There was no way I could stay here even if he had agreed to be the one to leave. Tears clouded my vision as I rushed down the stairs, stopping in the kitchen to grab some Advil and a glass of water. My hands shook with frustrated rage as I filled a glass at the sink.

Had *she* been in my kitchen?

Drank from my glasses?

Eaten off the plates we'd picked out together?

I slammed the glass down to the countertop, onto the lovely grey granite we'd chosen together five years ago when we'd remodeled the kitchen. We were happy five years ago. *Weren't we?*

Was anything real? And why was I so upset when I had planned to leave him anyway?

Oh yeah.

The humiliation.

The younger, blonder, boobier, secretarial cheating situation that had made my life into a cliché.

I was about to be gossiped about *so hard.*

My heart pounded in my ears as my breath grew shallow. Forget Advil—I needed my migraine prescription and a dark room. But the pills were upstairs in the bathroom currently occupied by my husband's secretary-slash-mistress.

And my bedroom? *Ew.*

I had to get out of here. But I had *nowhere to go.*

I had tolerated the little digs about my coffee shop, my body, my*self* that he'd dished my way over the last few years. I did it for my boys, to keep our family together. I'd put up with it until I couldn't do it anymore. But this was *beyond too much.*

I choked on a sob and swiped my hand under my

eyes to catch the tears, wincing as the overhead light caught on my rings. A gold wedding band, the tiny speck of a diamond engagement ring Tom had proposed with, and on top, the three huge diamonds he had insisted I wear when he felt he'd finally made it. I used to enjoy seeing them sitting pretty on my hand, a little reminder of the family we had created together and how far we had come when no one thought we would last. I extended my hand out to look one last time before slipping them off and placing them on the counter. All the while memories—happy, sad, and everything in between—swirled around me as my eyes darted over the house. This was like a death. My life as I had known it was over, and it was flashing before my eyes.

I slammed my eyes shut and collapsed on one of the bar stools at the island to rest my cheek against the cool granite, just for a minute. I needed to get the pounding in my head to stop before I left. My heart raced and grew burdened with sudden stress as it sank inside my body.

I had been planning my exit.

I wanted a divorce.

What in the frick was wrong with me?

"Oh, honey. Don't become a cliché. A sad, scorned little woman." Bethany grinned at me as she swanned down the stairs. Clearly, she thought she had won a great prize in Tom. Sure, he had oodles of money, a nice car, and this huge house in town. He had all the necessary requirements one looks for whilst digging for gold. But she had missed one pertinent fact: she was destined to become *me*, and *he* would eventually find somebody to replace *her*. The circle of life for cheating assholes.

I ignored her. Nothing I could say would get rid of that smug, smackable look on her face, and I wasn't willing to expend the effort on a catfight. He wasn't worth it, and I was beginning to wonder if he ever had been. I stood up and grabbed my purse.

"Bye now," she said with the bitchy smirk she always gave me whenever I saw her in Tom's office or my coffee shop.

I muttered under my breath as I left, "Just wait until he cheats on you, dumbass."

I had some of my headache prescription in my office. I could hide out in there until I decided where to go for the night, or until school let out and I had to tell the boys. Their relationship with their dad was already on shaky ground; this would make the bottom drop out from underneath it. My boys weren't completely oblivious to what went on in this house, no matter how hard I had tried to cover it up or brush it away with jokes and deflection. Our family therapist was making a fortune off my guilt and inability to just freaking leave.

Without sparing her another look, I found my keys on the table and headed to the front door. If she wanted him, she could have him. How long would it take until he started running her down like he'd been doing to me over the last few years? I almost felt sorry for her, but her motivations had been clear since the moment I'd met her, so I was okay with letting her reap what she had oh so carefully sewn.

I'm was done with him. Finally.

D-O-N-E. Done.

I slammed the door behind me as I left and immediately regretted it when my head started pounding again. Startled, I looked up and saw a car pull up to the curb with a squeal a split second before a large man jumped out.

Jake.

Headed my way with a face like thunder, storming up the front walkway as I drifted down. "Violet, I have to tell you something and this isn't going to be easy to hear—"

"Not now. I have to get out of here." I tried to step to the side to go around him, but he blocked my path with his tall, broad frame, and angry energy.

His eyes softened as they met mine and I quickly looked away. Sympathy would only make me start crying again. "This is important, and it's about Tom. I don't know how to tell you this—"

"What? That he's been cheating on me with Bethany for the last six months?"

He inhaled a sharp breath. "Six months? That long? Shit."

"Is that what you wanted to tell me?" I crossed my arms and stared up at him.

"Yes. I've been one step behind you all morning. I saw them together about an hour ago. Kissing in the parking lot of—"

"It doesn't even matter. I saw them myself, Jake. Right in my bed. But—" I looked up, seeing his soft blue eyes gleaming with sympathy and care as I met them with mine. "Thank you. I mean, you're his best friend. I appreciate that you were going to tell me and not try to cover for him."

He snorted. "I don't give a shit about Tom. *You're* my friend. Don't you know that by now? Tom can go to hell."

We both jumped as the front door opened. Tom and Bethany stepped out onto the porch, dressed for the workday and bearing Tom's bags packed for their ski trip. "Moretti! Hey, buddy," Tom called, sounding like it was just a normal day.

"Hey?" Jake's face showed his incredulity as he threw his arms out to the side. "That's it? Are you crazy, doing this so publicly? I saw you kissing her in front of your office. And I wasn't the only one. Don't you have any respect for your family?" My jaw dropped. I had yet to contemplate which side our friends would each land on when the news got out. I was happy Jake chose mine. He was a good man and the boys had always adored him.

"I sent her an email—"

Jake huffed out a hostile laugh. "An email? Are you fucking serio—"

"I have to go." I darted around him, trying to ignore their angry words. I hopped in my vehicle and started it but slammed to a stop halfway out of the driveway when I saw Tom attempt to shove Jake off the porch. Jake shook him off and turned around. He strode angrily to my car, tapping on my window when he arrived. I rolled it down, then rested my hand on the frame as I turned in my seat.

"I want you to call me if you or the boys need

anything. Any time, day or night, you can call me. Do you hear me, Violet?" His anger melted away as he spoke. His smile grew gentle as he studied my face.

"Yes, Jake," I murmured, still shaken from their confrontation on the porch.

His eyebrows knitted with concern. "I mean it. I'm going to call you tonight to check on you and the boys, and you'd better answer."

"Okay. I'll answer." I breathed.

He echoed my "*Okay*" with a soft whisper, then covered my hand briefly with his before taking it away. "You drive carefully. Is Holly still going to be at the shop when you get there?"

I nodded.

"That's good. You shouldn't be alone today. I'll talk to you tonight—in fact, I'll swing by and drop off dinner for you and the boys. Will you be here at the house or—?"

"I'll be here. I have to pack."

Storm clouds filled his eyes again. "That bastard . . . We'll talk more later." He pressed the pocket square from his suit jacket into my palm. "Just in case you need it on the way. Bye, sweetheart."

"Goodbye, Jake." I managed to say. I watched as he got into his car and drove away. Then I got out of there.

What the hell was that?

Heart to Heart

Just friends.
That's all Liam Carter and I can ever be.

Sure, we've shared a kiss or two and our chemistry is off
the charts.
And yeah, he's too hot to be real and he looks at me like
I'm the only woman in the world...

Pretending I don't want to date him when he's the
sweetest man I've ever met is almost impossible.

But I can't have him.

After what he went through, he deserves a fairytale.
And I'm bad at love, with the reputation to match.
Add those to the rest of the reasons why I should keep my
distance.
But here's the big one:

Did I mention we work together now?

I'm the hot mess trying to start up a new business and he's the got-it-all-together contractor in charge of the renovation.

The more time we spend together, the more I want—until I want it all.

How am I supposed to resist him now?

Available Now!

Chapter 1

There she was.

I hovered in the back of the long line for my daily hit of caffeine surreptitiously watching as she bustled around the espresso machine. I caught her eye and grinned as her cheeks turned red and she quickly looked away.

Violet's Café in Sweetbriar, Oregon, had become somewhat of a sanctuary for me since moving to town a few months back. The coffee was addicting, but that wasn't the main attraction anymore. Holly Barrett, the little sister of the owner, had caught my eye at first sight when she'd returned to town soon after I'd arrived, and I hadn't been able to look away ever since.

I refused to think about how many months I had been here or how long I'd been silently pining over the gorgeous blonde behind the counter. After my medical discharge from the Army, I vowed never to be bound by a clock or a schedule that I didn't create for myself ever again. My therapist's words floated through my mind as the line slowly moved through the shop.

To better spend your time, start by understanding where your time is spent.

Long line today or not, hopeless crush tearing up my heart or not, I liked it here. Time felt different here. Hours could pass and feel like nothing at all. Violet's coffee shop was heaven on earth, especially to someone who'd been stuck in a desert and bound by somebody else's rules for the last decade. The happy chaos of this place—not to mention the delicious smells, friendly faces, and homey feel—soothed me in a way I never wanted to lose. It was the polar opposite of the life I had known before I came to Sweetbriar.

Plus, as an entertaining bonus, this place had seen some *shit*. Town gossip, relationship dramas, jet-lagged travelers, ski-bums passing through on their way up the mountain, and the best part, the Barrett family themselves: boisterous, loving, and loud.

The line moved at a slow but steady pace. It was early afternoon, and Holly was the only barista behind the counter. It wasn't usually this busy at this time of day, but I didn't mind the wait, not when I had something as beautiful as her to look at.

"Finally," a deep voice boomed, and I tensed, ready to —what?

Nothing, stand down. He's probably harmless.

"I've been dying to see you all day, Holly." His tone

turned flirty, and the muscles in my jaw ticked as I listened to him hit on her, ready to step in if he took it too far. Or maybe I'd step in anyway. She was obviously not interested and there was something about him I didn't like.

"Sorry for the wait." She brushed her hands down the front of her half-apron, ignoring his come-on as she faced him. "What can I get for you today, Jared?"

"So many things, babe. But we'll start with the usual, a cappuccino. And I'd like to add that date I've been asking about."

Between my teeth grinding together hard enough to hurt and the possessive rage blinding me as I watched him chat her up, I knew I was only kidding myself when it came to being *just friends* with Holly.

"I can't. I, um—" she murmured while stammering over her words and avoiding his eyes. She was sweet and I had the sense that hurting someone's feelings by saying "no" wasn't easy for her.

"So, listen." He barreled on, ignoring the not-so-subtle hints she was giving him. "I want your number, babe. I'll take you to dinner in the city, then maybe to a club? I remember how much you liked to dance back in high school."

"I—like I told you before, I'm not in the right head space for dating right now, okay? I have a lot going on. It's not you, it's a me thing. I need to get settled back in town, and I still—"

"Aw, come on. Any head space you're in is fine with

me, and I bet I can settle you down." He reached across the counter and pulled her cell from the half apron tied around her waist. "I want your number."

"Jared!" Shocked, she jumped back, and I lurched forward, snatching the phone from his hand before he could get her number from it.

"Watch it. She said no." I passed it back to Holly, shoulder-checking him to the side as I stepped between him and the counter. She managed a tremulous smile as she mouthed, "Thank you," and took it, tucking it into her back pocket with a pointed glance toward a deliberately oblivious Jared.

"Oh really? She did?" Huffing a humorless laugh, he glared at me. "Because I didn't hear a '*no*'. I heard a 'not right now' or at the very least a 'maybe another time'. He turned back to her with a smarmy grin that I was *this close* to knocking off his face. "Sorry, babe. We'll make plans later." After stuffing a wad of cash in the tip jar, he took his order and stormed out.

I was last in line and despite the wait, the shop was fairly empty as most folks had taken their orders to go. A few customers lingered in the corner happily chatting. A quick glance showed they either hadn't noticed what had transpired or didn't want to intervene. "If I was out of line by stepping in—I mean, what he did is not okay, and if you'd wanted to tell him off yourself or maybe smack him around a little bit, I'm sorry—"

"Don't apologize. It's okay, I'm usually pretty good about taking care of myself. I wasn't expecting him to do anything like that. I've known him since kindergarten, he's always been pushy but harmless. Plus, I owe him for —it's a long, dumb, convoluted story but you might as well hear it from me. Basically, he saved me from making a huge mistake. My fiancé was a cheater and he let me know about it. Hence the Holly-left-a-guy-at-the-alter crap that sometimes goes around town about me, among other things." She stopped short in frustration. "I don't want to talk about Jared. *Gah,* I'm sorry, Liam. What'll it be?" she asked, as if she didn't tease me every day about ordering the same thing.

I smiled softly. "Why don't you surprise me this time?" I'd be keeping an eye on that prick. My protective hackles were up. But for now, I just wanted to make her feel better.

The heavy lashes that shadowed her freckled cheeks flew up in surprise. "Really?"

"Yeah, but nothing too sweet, I—"

Our eyes met. "Shh." Holding up a finger, she grinned. "I know what you'll like."

She didn't know even half of what I'd like from her.

My mouth turned up at the corner. "Okay, show me what you got."

She turned, reaching high on the shelf behind the counter for two glasses before filling them with ice. Stifling a groan, I watched her shirt rise up to bare a sliver of skin. I guess I was staying here for my coffee, and I didn't mind one bit.

Shoving my lust-fueled thoughts to the back of my

mind, I forced myself to stop watching her gorgeous ass as she worked and raised my gaze. But it was useless when the sight was not only burned onto my retinas but also into my senses. I slammed my eyes shut as I forced the memory of having my hands on that ass out of my head. We had kissed a few weeks back and it had been driving me to distraction ever since.

Violet threw a Valentine's Day party in the shop every year and for the latest one she'd come up with the bright idea to use balloons as a Valentine's version of Christmas mistletoe. Holly and I had found ourselves beneath a dozen or so and had made the most of it in the back room. It had happened in a rush of sensation and surprise and the feeling that I finally had somewhere to belong again, but it hadn't lasted.

"I'm not ready to jump into anything," she had said after. So I agreed to be her friend and held off asking her on a real date. We hadn't talked about it since. Deep down I knew I wasn't ready for anything serious either; I was still recovering from my time in the Army, among other things. The trouble was my heart didn't seem to agree with my head and logic went out the window whenever I got near her. The way my body jolted with electricity every time we got close made it glaringly obvious that I had feelings for her. But unlike Jared, the deluded dickhead who just left, I knew how to listen.

Just friends . . .

I let out a sigh, watching as she pulled a shot of espresso, then forced my myself to stop remembering our kiss as she prepared my drink. I had to distract myself; the direction my thoughts were going in was treacherous.

"Taste this." She dropped a straw into the glass then slid it across the counter with a sexy wink. I almost groaned out loud. Friends didn't wink at each other, did they? Or at least they shouldn't. But maybe it was my lingering thoughts about our kiss that made the wink sexy, and she hadn't intended it to be. Damn, I was a mess over her.

I raised the glass to my lips, my eyebrows popping up as the flavor hit my tongue. "What is this?"

"It's sugar-free, so no worries." She waved a hand up and down in front of me. "I know how you like to keep things healthy." It was true, I was somewhat of a health nut. "But I've noticed your weekly cinnamon muffin indulgence, hence the drink. You like?"

"It tastes like when I dunk the muffin in my coffee, except it's iced. Delicious." I took another sip, nodding in appreciation.

"Exactly." One shoulder shrugged up as her pretty eyes sparkled with satisfaction. "For some reason, it's not as good hot. It's my favorite despite its healthy qualities. Normally I have the eating habits of a stoned raccoon at a full dumpster, but Vi was experimenting with healthier drink options last week and now I'm hooked." She placed a straw in her glass and took a sip for emphasis.

I chuckled. "Well, this might turn out to be my new favorite too. Sit with me?" I invited without thinking. "The rush is gone; you could take a break."

Her cute nose wrinkled up in uncertainty. "Do you really think we should?"

"What happened on Valentine's Day, stays on Valentine's Day. Right?" I cajoled with a grin.

"Right," she confirmed with a laugh. "Holiday hall pass."

"Yup." I gestured to the sofa in the corner then headed that way. Heat surged through my veins when I heard her footsteps clicking over the wood floor behind me. "Besides, I think it's World Compliment Day. I heard it on the radio on the way to work this morning." I turned and gave her a wink of my own. "We should be okay to have coffee together. Holiday hall pass and all that . . ."

"Really? What a cute idea for a holiday." She sat on the brown leather armchair perpendicular to the couch. "Well, you look very handsome today, Liam. In honor of the holiday, of course."

I sat and held up my glass in her direction. "And you're as gorgeous as ever."

Obviously, it hadn't escaped my attention that she'd made two drinks when I asked her to sit with me. *Was taking a break with me her plan all along?*

I studied her face but, as usual, it was inscrutable. I decided not to question my good fortune and just enjoy her company. She was a fascinating mix of wide open, heart on her sleeve, friendliness, and hot-as-fuck innocent flirtation, and I was the fool dangling on her hook like a hapless fish with a semi-hopeless crush.

"Why, thank you, kind sir. Cheers to holidays and good friends." She tapped her glass to mine. "I should have grabbed some muffins or a cookie. Or would that have been overkill, Mr. Healthy?" she teased.

"No, not overkill. But it would've definitely spoiled my dinner." A blond curl escaped her loose ponytail when she laughed, and I wanted to tuck it behind her ear. I wanted to take that rubber band out and get my hands in her hair again. God, it was soft. It had felt like silk in my palms when we kissed.

I knew I should stop looking at her as though we stood a chance. As if I could ever be good for her with all my baggage, but I couldn't stop myself. She was like sunshine, and I was starved for more of her light.

"What's for dinner tonight? Do you cook? We never covered that topic on Valentine's Day."

"I can. I used to cook dinner with my mom every night until she, um . . ." *Died. Why did everything in my past have to be such a downer?*

"Liam . . ." Her voice was gentle as if she knew my history, and maybe she did. Her brother-in-law, Luke, was my best friend. I'd followed him to Sweetbriar after leaving the Army and he was the reason I was still here.

I shrugged, not wanting to bring her down. "Yeah, I'm not opposed to sweets, and I can cook pretty much everything. I'm just not quite at stoned-raccoon level."

Her knowing eyes held mine with that warmth and that light that I needed so badly in my life. "Well, I don't cook, as you know." Her mouth quirked up at the corner and she leaned in as if to confess something terrible. "You should see Levi and Jude and me at dinner time. If we're not running home to mooch off our parents, we're nuking crap food in the microwave or ordering pizza like a bunch of frat boys." She blew out a sigh and that loose curl went flying. "I need to get my own place. I need to learn a few more life skills, too. God, I need to just grow up. How sad is it that I have to crash with my younger brothers? I'm almost thirty and I sleep on their couch, Liam. *Ugh.*"

"It's not sad at all. Look, you just got back to town. As you said before, you need time to settle in, to find your footing here again. Don't forget your accomplishments— your travel blog, your photography. You touched a lot of people with your stories, Holly. Including me."

Her head tilted as she offered me a soft smile. "You're kind. Thank you for saying that." Back on Valentine's Day, I told her I had followed her online. I read her blog, followed her on Instagram, and kept up with her submissions to the various magazines and websites that published her work as best I could. She'd brushed past my admission, thanking me, but not letting the conversation get deep enough to allow me to express what her work had meant to me. She was talented but I had the feeling she didn't realize how much.

"I didn't say that just to be kind. In fact, I should thank you for the homeopathic stuff you used to share. Sadly, those posts came in handy way too often." I held my arm out to show her the burn scar running up the back. "Exhibit A."

She took my arm, turning it side to side. "Oh man, that must have hurt."

"It would have been worse, but I used that mixture with—" She ran her fingertips over my scar, and I shivered. Like I'd been sucker punched, the sudden need for more of her touch roared in my ears and I lost my words as I imagined her hand on my arm in an entirely different scenario. *Gripping, clutching, nails digging in as I—.*

"The calendula one?"

Hastily, I nodded and drew my arm back. "Yes, that's the one."

Her nose scrunched up as she watched me. Why did she have to be so cute? As if being stunningly gorgeous wasn't enough, she also had to be adorable.

"You look flushed," she told me.

I inhaled a sharp breath as the back of her hand went to my forehead before drifting down to my cheek. "I'm fine."

"Maybe you're coming down with something."

I shook my head and kept my mouth shut because nothing appropriate would come out when *you, me,* and *right now* were the only words running through my mind.

This was impossible. I'd had my hands on her body and my mouth on her lips, her neck, and that sweet little spot behind her ear that might become one of my favorites if given another chance to explore her. I'd come so close to getting everything I wanted, but I couldn't have it.

Yet.

Knock it off.

She wasn't ready for more and I was going to respect that. It was the right thing to do.

"I'll be okay. Maybe I'll go to bed early tonight," I finally answered. "I'm probably just tired." *Tired—the* universal excuse for everything. I stifled a chuckle at my own expense.

I used to imagine what it would be like to be near her, to talk to her, to touch her. And now I knew. Half of me wished I'd never found out, while the other half yearned to discover even more.

Available Now!

Change of Heart

He's Sweetbriar's most devoted cop, my ex-husband, and
the man I've avoided for the last ten years.
He might also be my only hope.

Cade Barrett was my first crush, my first kiss, my first
everything.
I thought we'd last forever.
But we wanted different things out of life.
He was a hometown boy through and through,
While my ambitions reached far beyond our small town.

So we let each other go and I left to chase my dreams.
Now I'm back with a secret—the dangerous kind.
He vowed to keep me safe.
While I promised myself to guard my heart.

Until one accidental kiss reignited the fire between us.
And it was hotter than ever before.

Will one final night together extinguish the flames?
Or should I stay and take the one and only chance I have
to get him back?

One and Only is now titled Change of Heart!
Same Cade and Charlotte with a BRAND NEW
EPILOGUE!
Available NOW!

Chapter 1

Cade

I blinked against the silvered glare of the sun on the snow packed road, yawning as I drove. Twelve-hour shifts sucked but working one overnight was the worst. I was exhausted, hungry, and ready to get into bed with the leftover pizza in my fridge and my Netflix account before crashing into a comatose oblivion. I stretched in my seat and continued up the highway into the mountains. Sweetbriar, Oregon, was one of the small towns you'd pass through on your way to Mount Hood. My house was located up in the foothills overlooking town. And thankfully, I was almost there.

"Slow down, damn it," I muttered as a Range Rover passed me, hitting a hidden patch of black ice and fish-tailing side to side before regaining control. The out-of-state plates let me know how clueless they were about the danger they were in. Plus, what kind of dumbass passes a cop?

My head whipped to the side as a Subaru sped around me, driving right up to the bumper of the Range Rover. "What the hell?"

I switched my lights and siren on, hoping it would suffice as a warning as it was too slick for a pursuit. It was ski season, and the roads were full of vacationers with no clue how to drive in the snow. I couldn't put the other vehicles at risk by chasing these two boneheads down. On a day like this, just being out on the roads was hazardous enough. A police chase between three cars would wreak more havoc than letting them go. But I called it in to the station so everyone would be on the lookout and hoped I wouldn't come across their mangled wreckage further up the highway.

I was not in the mood for that kind of paperwork.

All I had wanted was to go home, have a snack, and crash. But I had an ominous feeling that wasn't going to happen. The crackle of my radio interrupted my thoughts and I cursed.

The voice of the dispatcher on duty asked, "Cade, do you copy?"

"Yeah, unfortunately."

"I'm sorry, but you're the closest. There's a crash, single vehicle. Uh, the Range Rover you just called in a few minutes ago. Right by the turn-off to your place."

"I'm almost there." I sighed.

"Ambulance and fire are on the way."

I grunted. My day was ruined before it had even started. Or, ended, as the case may be.

The Ponderosa pine at the edge of my property had borne the brunt of the crash. I arrived in time to see the driver exit the vehicle, stumbling out to fall forward into the snow. Long golden-brown waves covered her face as she rose to her hands and knees trying to gain purchase on the slippery surface. I pulled off to the side, turned off the siren but left the lights flashing, and got out.

"Hey, hold still, you could be hurt. I'm coming to help you!" I shouted as I made my way closer.

Clearly panicked, she lurched for the open door of her vehicle and pulled herself up. "Stay away from me!" The door hit my shoulder as she attempted to close it.

"Ma'am, it's okay, you're safe. I'm Detective Caden Barrett, Sweetbriar PD. I'm here to help. An ambulance is on the way."

"Cade?" With a shaking hand, she pushed the thick mass of waves from her face. Gorgeous baby-blue eyes met mine before she burst into tears and fell into my arms. "Oh, thank goodness it's you."

"Charlotte." Shocked was not the right word for how it felt to be holding her again. A jolt of electricity lit me up inside and I gasped, ruffling her hair with my breath. I inhaled deeply, her sweetly familiar floral scent filling my nostrils, and before I could think too hard about it, I pulled her close, tugging her tight against my chest. That same heady rush of sensation shot through my body at the feel of her soft curves finally beneath my hands again. "Are you hurt?" Goosebumps traveled over my flesh as she wrapped her arms around me and pressed herself even closer. Trembling fingers drifted into the hair at the nape of my neck, and I shivered at her touch.

"No. I'm okay, I think. Just shaken up. I wasn't going that fast when I hit our tree, but the airbag went off." I swallowed hard, trying to steel myself against the rush of memories that currently threatened my good sense. I didn't want to let her go but I had no reason to keep her close.

Soft hands went to my shoulders, pushing me away as she stepped back to lean against the side of the Range Rover. Visible just over her shoulder, the heart I'd carved into the bark when we had first bought this place taunted me. I should have carved an X through it after she left. Or chopped the damn thing down.

"This isn't your car. Where's your Jeep? Why were you driving so fast?" I questioned her. "Was that Subaru following you?" I peppered her with questions about the crash to avoid talking to her about anything real.

Why, after all this time, have you come back to Sweetbriar?

Why did you leave me?

She avoided my eyes as she answered. "No, uh, I mean, I have no idea. Maybe it was road rage? Or they probably thought I was somebody else—"

Blaring sirens filled the air as the fire department's ambulance pulled up next to us, followed by a squad car and a firetruck. Frustrated, I turned to find my younger brother, Levi, stepping out of the driver's side of the ambulance followed by his partner. "Charlotte? Is that you?" His smile was huge as he approached us. "Are you okay? Hey, Cade." I nodded hello to Levi and scowled as Matt, a fellow Sweetbriar PD officer, approached. My moment with Charlotte was obviously over.

Matt called out with a smile, "Yo, Cade, go home and get some sleep. We got it from here."

"Fine. Great. Thanks. Charlotte?" My heart ached as I watched her trembling in the cold. She was as beautiful as ever: freckles on her nose, full pink lips, curves for days, and that same delicate vulnerability that had always hit me straight in the middle of my damn chest every time her eyes had caught mine. Why I wanted to be the one to help her, I did not fully understand, not when she'd so thoroughly smashed my heart beneath her shoe when she walked out of my life over a decade ago.

She looked away. All she said was a meek, "Thank you, Cade."

Levi draped a blanket over her shoulders and led her to the ambulance. She was in good hands with him. I turned my back and headed for my SUV. Of *course* that's all she had to say. I was lucky she'd spoken to me at all, seeing as how we'd been divorced for so long. Not to mention the fact that she had married and divorced someone else during our time apart.

On a giant exhale, I jumped into my car, started it, and drove through the gate adjacent to the Ponderosa pine currently getting way more attention from her busted Range Rover than she'd just given me.

I had known Charlotte was back. You can't live in a town as small as this one and not know all the comings and goings, especially in my line of work. But we'd made an art of avoidance over the last decade; this was only the second time I'd had any contact with her since our divorce. It wasn't easy given both our families were long-time Sweetbriar residents and had known each other for years, but fortunately, everyone was still civil with one another.

Charlotte and I had gone from preschool through graduation together and I had known her brothers almost as well as I knew my own siblings. Her family owned an auto body and mechanic shop right outside of town and I was probably the only person in in the area who didn't bring my vehicles to their place. In fact, I hadn't seen any of her family in years except in passing.

After trudging through the snow in my driveway, I made it to my porch. I could see the roof of the coffee shop owned by my older sister, Violet, from here. I should have stopped and grabbed breakfast from her. The thought of cold pizza now turned my stomach, and Netflix? Forget about it. I was too keyed up to relax and I had no one to chill with.

Heaving out a sigh, I unlocked my door and went inside. After kicking off my boots, I headed for the kitchen. My feet slowed over the tile as I approached the island in the center. Palms to my head, I turned in a slow circle. "Damn it," I growled to the empty room, slamming my eyes shut as images of me and Charlotte together burned in the back of my mind. Fucking hell, there was no way I could sleep now, and I had lost my appetite.

I didn't have time for this.

For her or the memories I had worked so hard over the years to banish from my mind.

Or for anything that didn't involve my path toward taking over as chief of police from my father when he retired, which, given the way my mother was pushing him, would be sooner than later.

Why did she have to come back when I'd finally gotten over her? I stalked to my bathroom, tearing my clothes off on the way. A hot shower was what I needed, then I'd go to bed *without* remembering all the nights I'd spent buried inside of her sweet little body, the vows we'd taken, the promises we'd made, the dreams we had shared . . . And I couldn't forget the plans—years' worth of plans—for our future, dead and buried, gone with the stroke of a pen.

The hot spray of water did nothing to calm me down. I turned it to cold, shivering beneath the icy blast as I hurried to wash this entire day away. Trying to scrub thoughts of her out of my mind was useless when I could still feel the soft press of her body against mine.

After slipping into my robe, I cranked up the heater, bypassing my bedroom to fall back on my couch with a plop. I stared at my reflection in the TV screen, my remote sitting beneath it across the room. There were some days when nothing went my way, and apparently this was one of them. On every level. I was well and good into a pity party for one when I punched a throw pillow, then fell to my side. I had just drifted off when pounding on my door woke me up.

"Damn. Seriously?"

"Yo, Cade! Let me in." It was Levi. If he didn't have food or coffee, he would not be invited inside.

Throwing open the door, I greeted him with a grouchy, "What?"

He waved a lavender bag in my face and pushed his way inside. "I brought breakfast from Violet. And a smoothie. You're welcome, sunshine." His knowing smirk was infuriating, but I'd let it go until after I ate. I headed to my room to dress.

His feet were on my coffee table and he was already stuffing his face when I made it back to the living room. Apparently, I had company to entertain.

"Why is your remote way over there, dumbass? Get it before you sit down. Then you can go ahead and ask me."

"Ask you what?" I chucked the remote to him before grabbing the bag full of breakfast he'd brought and taking a huge sip of smoothie. "Thanks, man."

His eyebrows went up as he sipped his coffee and chuckled at my pathetic attempt to keep my feelings to myself. "About Charlotte. She's fine, by the way. I drove her to her dad's place. Her brothers swarmed her like she was near death or something."

"I can imagine." They were probably driving her crazy. She grew up the youngest of six kids and she was the only girl.

"They'll tow her car out to the shop later. You doin' okay? This is the first time you've seen her since she's been home, right?"

"It's fine. I'm fine. I'm over it." I answered, swiping the remote out of his hand and flicking the TV on.

"Sure. Okay." His side eyed skepticism was warranted, but also annoying.

I huffed a beleaguered sigh and avoided his eyes. "I don't want to talk about her," I muttered.

"You never do, and that's fine. I'm only here to help."

"Not to pry?" I arched a brow.

He laughed. "I would never." Levi was a nosy little shit and always had been. He would pry eventually. My entire family was a bunch of meddlers, always up in each other's business. But not me; I stayed out of everyone's way, and I expected the same treatment.

"Mom didn't find out and send you over here?" I prodded. "Ever since she found out about all of it, she's been trying to get me to discuss the fact that Charlotte divorced her husband and asking how I feel about her being single and back in town." I sent him a warning look. "I'm not talking about it, with any of you."

"I'm not here for that, okay?" His eyes softened in sympathy. "The look on your face at the crash site was intense is all. I was worried about you."

My eyebrows lifted in surprise. "Oh, well, thanks. I'm fine. Just tired. I worked all night." I wasn't sure if I wanted to be alone; my memories of Charlotte were coming at me like a freight train, and a distraction could be a good thing. But I was absolutely sure I didn't want to talk about anything that had happened this morning so I turned the volume up on the TV to discourage any more conversation.

About the Author

Nora Everly is a lifelong bookworm. She started reading the good stuff once she grew tall enough to sneak the romance novels off the top of her mother's bookshelf and it has been non-stop ever since.

Once upon a time she was a substitute teacher and an educational assistant. Now she's a writer and stay at home mom to two small humans and one fat cat.

Nora lives in the Pacific Northwest with her family and her overactive imagination.

Find her at noraeverly.com
Join the Nora News mailing list:
https://www.noraeverly.com/newsletter-1

Also by Nora Everly

The Sweetbriar Mountain Series:

Smartypants Romance:

Star Crossed Lovers (As Piper Everly):

Made in the USA
Monee, IL
07 January 2025

76289365R00069